STRAINED SIGMA BONDS

ARASIBO CAMPECHE

For JAM

ACKNOWLEDGMENTS

LIKE MANY WORTHWHILE PURSUITS, thinking is a community activity. I started writing in 2014 while trying to find something to do that was cheap, didn't require buying equipment, or worse, physical exercise, and that I could continue improving upon for the rest of my life. There were a few candidates but after mentioning it to a fellow lab mate, he mentioned that I should pick up writing. At that point, I wasn't aware that short fiction venues publishing SF/F existed. I thought it over as I kept doing experiments in a small windowless lab, and after a few months gave it a go.

I started by reading Golden Age science fiction alongside extant magazines and wrote what I thought at the time were genius stories. They were not. I soon realized I was going nowhere fast and reached out to a few editors. Awesome writer and editor Nick Mamatas ended up being my first teacher. It took a while, but I made my first sale to Daily Science Fiction in 2017. A few years later, I benefited from my second teacher, Lucy Snyder. Both Nick and Lucy deserve more credit for this collection being published than I can articulate.

This collection wouldn't exist without the support and inspiration from friends and family. I will not list them here, since I'll forget someone and then lose sleep over it.

I'd like to also thank Steven Radecki and the rest of the team at Water Dragon Publishing for believing in these stories enough to publish them. Two were already published in previous Dragon Gems anthologies, which are full of amazing stories. And thanks to Danielle Fine for the great cover.

While I have put countless hours into becoming a better writer and always strive to think more clearly, I should also acknowledge a very important part of anyone's success, a little daimon that patiently waits in the shadows, ready to pop out when most needed: Luck.

CONTENTS

PENALTIES OF ENTROPY

Four days before impact

THE STARS LOOKED LIKE they were melting. Gustavo sat, eyes filled with tears, on the leeward side of the ship, a few inches of high-temperature quartz glass between him and the vacuum of space.

The ship's hull creaked and moaned as it left the cold temperatures of empty space. Had there been windows on the other side of the ship, he'd be able to see himself on a crash course with a solar analog, where'd he'd be killed by either ionizing radiation or cooked to death, depending on how the silica fibers insulating the hull fared.

He turned from the window and stood in front of his cluttered lab bench, waiting for a miracle.

The physicists at the Nikola space station were celebrated as the smartest people in their field and had calculated and recalculated his ship's trajectory—which involved a parabolic route starting from the space station and ending in a distal pickup point—considering every risk and problematic parameter. The ship was on autopilot; there was no manual control, no tweaking its course. No escape. The risk of accidents during these missions was significant but worth it, at least until an accident actually happened.

If he discovered a new organism, Gustavo could get a cushy professor job in any biology department on Earth and spend the next twenty years milking that one time he went to space.

The samples on his bench, milligrams of space debris he'd hoped were populated by previously undiscovered microbes, sat dead. After growing dust samples on dozens of rich media, he determined none contained life. This was before he found out he'd die on this ship.

Gustavo paced around the lab. He cried and screamed for hours, begging to be saved.

Between bouts of retching, footsteps echoed behind him. At first, he'd been afraid and locked himself in the bathroom. Later, he made peace with the fact he was hallucinating and did his best to ignore the man that had appeared out of nowhere.

•　　•　　•

Three days to impact

The ship shuddered and woke Gustavo. He'd been asleep for twelve hours, and in three days, he'd be dead. Sleeping was a waste of time he could spend looking for solutions.

The university would send a search party when they received his emergency probes and maybe find residue of his ship that didn't instantaneously atomize. They'd declare him deceased. Lisa would cry, then struggle to explain to their daughter Joana what death was, then tell her that daddy was now dead.

Gustavo made his way to the fitness room and ran for as long as he could on the treadmill. The screen in front of him had stopped receiving signals. They had probably been distorted by the radiation from the solar analog. There were no more news updates, video calls with Lisa and Joana, or tongue-in-cheek messages from his boss asking if he'd discovered something to make them famous. Outgoing signals were also blocked as far as he could tell, but he still had to try. After running until his legs refused to continue, he sat in the communication room and tried to hail home.

"This is Gustavo Pereira. There was an error in my mapped trajectory. I am headed for the center of a solar analog. My navigation station burned out, and I can't tell how far this star is from the space station. Tell Lisa and Joana that ..."

He took a deep breath and cut off the microphone. He'd already spent enough time crying in his messages. He imagined Lisa listening to the recordings over and over after he was dead; hearing his despair wouldn't make it better for her.

He bashed the communication console with the fire extinguisher until the instrumentation lay in pieces. Partly, he didn't need it anymore and enjoyed sweating for a bit, but really, he just craved the euphoria that comes from destroying expensive equipment. It was like breaking something that was otherwise unbreakable—not because of the item's constitution, but because who would think of breaking it?

He sat back in the chair, catching his breath and reveling in the chaos. He took a moment to enjoy the pleasure of taboo destruction.

•   •   •

"I'm not a hallucination. I'm a demon, but not in a bad way, so you can stop ignoring me. My name is Pierre."

Gustavo dropped an Eppendorf tube, bent down to get it, and hit his head on the lab bench on his way up.

"I thought you would go away," Gustavo said.

"I'll go away soon," Pierre said. "I know everything. You should enjoy our conversations instead of doing work with the little time you have."

"How can I save myself?" Gustavo asked. There was no way this would work. Engaging with hallucinations was like talking to yourself.

"There is no way with the time you have left. What do you think you'll miss the most from being alive?"

"Stop talking," Gustavo said, sitting at the LC-MS system's computer.

"What are you looking for?" Pierre asked.

Claiming he knew everything was ridiculous enough in itself. The fact that Pierre asked so many questions only made the claim more stupid. Why ask so many questions if you knew everything?

Pierre sat at the far end of the lab bench. Gustavo could only see the demon out of the corner of his eye but knew he was smiling.

Gustavo used a thin steel spatula to scoop up a few hundred micrograms of the space dust he'd collected during his assignment. There were two straightforward explanations for what was happening. Either his mind was trying to give him companionship to soothe the last few days of his life, or the samples were not stored correctly, and he'd been exposed to hallucinogens. Despite having only a few days left, he needed to know; not knowing was an itch he couldn't ignore.

"Why don't you tell me what I'm looking for?" Gustavo asked.

"I can't read your thoughts." Pierre stood and shrugged. He was wearing a button-down shirt with the top two buttons open, the sleeves rolled up to the elbow. Instead of a demon, he looked more like an accountant sitting at a bar after a hard day of massaging spreadsheets.

"That's convenient," Gustavo said. He pipetted 1 milliliter of a 1:1 methanol:water solution into the vial containing the dust, tightened the cap, and mixed it using the benchtop vortex.

If he was lucky, some of the extracted compounds would hint at Pierre's origins.

"The problem is that I can't see the neurons shooting in your brain. Your mind is a black box. How am I supposed to know things without having access to the initial conditions that led to it? I'm not God."

"Are you the devil?" Gustavo asked, feeling a mixture of embarrassment and cleverness.

Pierre laughed. "Not *the* devil."

"Is the devil real?" Here was a yes or no question that would be in reach of an all-knowing, albeit limited, being. Gustavo was also curious. What if the devil was real and all-powerful, and enjoyed hurtling young scientists to their deaths?

"As real as you or me."

Gustavo shook his head, frustrated. Pierre was only questions and riddles. "That's what I'm trying to figure out."

"Ah, are you looking for derivatives of tryptophan or tyrosine that could be making me appear? I can tell you don't feel high. Are your thinking ergots, tryptamines? Not cannabinoids. You're not hungry."

Pierre's smile broadened like a child who'd been told they'd done a good job.

"That's exactly what I'm looking for. Good guess." Gustavo turned his back to Pierre, placed the vial on the sample tray, and started the mass spectrometer run. "Although, you did only guess after I nearly gave it away."

Pierre walked closer to the mass spectrometer and leaned forward. "What's happening inside is fascinating. Why did you build such a boring container?"

Despite the complicated physics, the instrument as a whole looked like a plastic box barely large enough to fit a person in the fetal position.

"Good question. And interesting," Gustavo said. Why hadn't his brain concocted a hallucination of a beautiful woman in a bikini?

Pierre nodded with wide eyes, ignoring his sarcasm. "The molecules are separated by polarity as they travel through the liquid chromatography column. They get ionized, and the charged radical species break down in an act of chemical violence."

"I know that. It's a high schooler's description of the process with a bit of poetry at the end," Gustavo said.

Pierre made his way back to the bench and stared at space samples and solvent bottles. "I know, you know. The broken molecules smashing into the detector are pieces of your parent molecule. The trick is to be able to reconstruct what you started with. You never actually detect what you started with ..."

Gustavo stood from the computer. "I get it. Please stop talking."

"You know, but you don't understand." Pierre shook his head. "What you don't understand is the foundation of how I come to know things."

Gustavo remained silent. He was curious as if he really was talking to another person. Was this the last stage of losing his mind? "How do you come to know things then?"

Pierre locked eyes with him. "I have knowledge because there is knowledge in destruction."

●   ●   ●

Pierre followed Gustavo everywhere, even in his dreams.

They were sitting in a dark room. The floor was coated in a thick, filmy substance resembling a bacterial biofilm. Gustavo knew that if he touched it, his skin would dissolve, mixing his atoms in the biofilm's matrix until the matter composing his body dispersed to form a colloid, as if his atoms were insoluble particles in a turbid suspension with the viscous goop.

A square stainless-steel table appeared between him and Pierre; this was the same material that made up both of their chairs. On the table was a deck of playing cards still in the box.

"This deck of cards has never been opened," Pierre said. He crossed his legs into the lotus position on the chair. Gustavo imitated him.

"The cards were randomized, instead of the typical order, they are boxed in. I don't have access to their history or how they were made. How much knowledge would I need to have now to tell you which card is in the front?"

Gustavo swallowed. "It's impossible."

"Exactly." Pierre blew on the deck and it vaporized, the air was foggy with the paper microparticles. The demon squinted and rubbed his hands together, eyes darting around like electrons orbiting an atom's nucleus. "It was the queen of hearts."

Gustavo awoke and recognized that Pierre was his mind's manifestation of Laplace's demon. The demon predicted everything based on previous knowledge. Gustavo couldn't believe such a creature existed. If the sequence of events was knowable, then they were predetermined, set in stone. But he'd chosen his path, to discover, to do science.

•　　•　　•

Gustavo was crying so much that the tears got into his mouth and snot ran down his nose. Food tasted saltier and was thicker. Swallowing scrambled eggs was like forcing wriggling worms down his throat. At the same time, knowing that this would be one of his last meals made eating a unique experience— his whole body felt engaged, challenged even, with every bite. This contradiction was probably what the death row inmates described in old novels felt like when having their last meal.

Pierre hadn't shown up today. Gustavo missed the demon, a fact which made him uncomfortable. After eating, he sat in his lab and went through the data he'd collected yesterday. The dust sample had thousands of masses in it. Some, like simple hydrocarbons, were easy to identify.

A few decades ago, it would have been astonishing to find small peptides or single amino acids floating in space, but after the first microbes, named cosmophiles, were found, no one cared about single molecules. Unless he returned with a new organism, preferably one resembling a single-celled eukaryote, he'd be one more scientist surveying space over and over again, trying to get lucky, sifting through dust, hoping for a career-making biological nugget. But manned missions had an expiration date; AI was becoming cheap enough that it would replace people soon enough.

Today he felt like making a difference, if not in his own life, maybe in someone else's. There was one rescue probe left. He'd already shot two into space, asking for help, but there was no point. By the time they came looking for him, his ship would have plunged into the solar analog with core temperatures in the tens of millions of degrees Celsius.

The probe had enough space for a message containing two thousand words, and instead of re-detailing his situation, Gustavo wrote a letter to Joana, so she could read it when she was older. The words didn't come. He tried to concentrate. Everything sounded like tired clichés.

I love you more than all the stars in space.

Take care of your mom. I know you'll grow up to be a wonderful woman.

You can be whatever you want when you grow up.

He deleted, rewrote, deleted again. Instead of what he'd done in life, he considered what he'd never done that would've been worthwhile. What would he have done differently in his life that could serve as honest advice? Since his teen years, he'd been aware, at least at some level, that life was a never-ending series of evaluations.

Don't do what I did: Get good grades in high school, go to a good college, then a good Ph.D. program, then a good postdoc position. I slept in cars, stole toilet paper from university bathrooms …

He thought of what else to write. About how before he knew it, he was living off of beer and cigarettes, how his scientific career came before his health, how his weekends were spent drinking and hungover.

But who wanted to read that much whining from the dead?

He deleted that and went back to the clichés. At the end he wrote: *You should do whatever makes you happy, whenever it makes you happy. The future is important, but life is short and not worth taking too seriously.*

He sent the probe.

"That reads okay to me," Pierre said from behind his shoulder. "She'll reference it when she receives her Nobel prize. Trust me."

•　　•　　•

Two days before impact

Gustavo zipped up his thermal shirt and started donning his space suit. The helmet clicked into place, and cool air started flowing from the pack on his back. If he created a large enough explosion after rupturing the fire extinguisher, he might push his ship to safety.

Pierre shook his head sadly. "This isn't going to work. It's like spitting out the window of a speeding car, hoping to give it enough momentum to change course. Stay here. I'll tell you what every single ion is in your data set from yesterday. I'll describe to you every single lifeform in the universe." The demon followed him to the ladder leading outside.

Learning about aliens tempted Gustavo to stay inside. After a pause, he kept climbing. At this point, it was clear that what Pierre wanted was for him to do nothing. Maybe the demon did know of a way that Gustavo could save himself and wasn't telling him. Gustavo had asked dozens of times to only receive noncommittal babble. Knowing everything is not the same as being honest.

The timer on Gustavo's wrist read: *45 hrs. 17 min. 33 sec.* He had almost two days to find out how to escape. In a way, the bleakness of his situation was freeing; any idea was fair game. The worst that could happen is that he accidentally killed himself and died a couple of hours early.

Gustavo stood on the shell plating with the fire extinguisher and drill in hand. The red metal didn't turn frosty, reminding him he was already in the solar analog's grasp. Indeed, the screen on his forearm read 200°C. He lay prone on the edge of the ship, hooked the fire extinguisher to the first nook he found, then drilled a hole in it while protecting his face. The extinguisher shattered in a noiseless explosion, propelling metal shards and a spray of CO_2. He quickly inspected his hand to make sure there were no cuts in his gloves and sat on the hull. He checked the ship's predicted path on the screen covering his forearm. No change.

His shoulders slumped. The star he was headed to was the size of a fist in the distance. What looked like whips of fire flayed on the surface. He closed his eyes and squeezed as hard as he could to stop the tears from flowing.

Pierre sat beside him, not wearing a spacesuit.

"I'm curious about the aliens, I admit it, but I'm angry and frustrated," Gustavo said. "I don't want to die. What good is knowing, if I'll die in two days?" Gustavo looked to the stars, thinking about how far they always looked, regardless of where you were in space.

"It won't always be like that. You can't let go of your ego, but it can be torn from you."

Gustavo heard yet didn't process what Pierre said.

"I don't want to die, "Gustavo said.

"You'll just change."

•   •   •

Day of impact

Yesterday, Gustavo had tried to pull the tall gas tanks in the lab up the ladder, but they were too heavy. Afterward, he poured all the methanol in the lab over the bench, opened the bottles of flammable solvents like hexane and ethyl acetate, then lit the lab on fire. Muffled explosions sounded through the steel door to his bedroom. The ship didn't change course.

Hours before impact, Gustavo sat on the floor, his back against the wall. His clothes were soaked in the sweat of stress and heat.

Pierre appeared from beside him and sat on a chair, looking him over.

"At what age would I have died if I didn't come here?" Gustavo asked.

"Thirty-four. And you die today," Pierre said. Gustavo's fantasy of having had the opportunity to live a different life ended before he could get lost in his imagination.

"What?" he asked.

Pierre smirked. "You die here. It couldn't have gone differently. The reason I know is that the past is the future of another point. What happened before determines what will happen next. Imagine a domino run with no start or end."

Gustavo cracked his neck slowly, focusing on the noises his body made. "You already said you can't read my mind because neurons fire randomly. If I can't predict my thoughts, how can I predict my actions?"

"You're only one person. If random events happen thousands or even millions of times, there's no way to predict. But when that number is closer to infinite, then the future averages out. Every single moment, there are an infinite number of events happening, molecules colliding with each other, events entangled with one another. In that movement, there is energy and violence, and information."

Gustavo was about to ask another question when his hands started itching. Smoke was rising from his palms. His hands turned red. The flesh underneath his epidermis was exposed as if he had washed his hands with acid.

In the rising ribbons of gaseous molecules, there was knowledge.

Lipid rafts danced in the air, dissociating to become individual fatty acids that broke down into individual molecules. He breathed in the smoke and knew that there was consciousness in atoms.

Pierre was sublimating, too—his face looked like God was a frustrated painter and had tried to erase his creation but only managed to smear it across space.

Gustavo knew the matter that once composed his body would spread across the universe, the atoms free to tumble in all dimensions, no longer hindered by the enthalpy that pulled his body together. He would meet Pierre again; perhaps they would be carbon atoms, cis to each other in isoprene, part of a community of millions that form natural rubber, or in a strained three-membered ring that formed cyclopropane, or maybe they would isomerize as part of the molecule called retinal, alkene bonds interchanging between cis and trans as light hit them to allow vision in mammals.

Gustavo could be a hydroxyl on a glucose molecule that drove ATP production in Joana!

He would be her guardian forever, her genius loci.

Gustavo knew everything, but there was so much left to feel, untapped dimensions of love and pleasure.

He took a deep breath, then exhaled a mist of lungs.

GIVEN PAIN, $\Delta S_{\text{UNIVERSE}} \geq 0$

THE DEMON SAT ATOP the white wall separating creation from nothingness. Her hair hung like bundled amyloid fibrils; her eyes were exploding stars.

She had long ago forgotten her age—she felt eternal—but the wall was older, and a mystery of its own.

Bubble-shaped universes floated before her like soft elastic marbles. She picked one at random and peered through dust and gas, through lipid membranes, atomic spins, then pulled back and focused on her favorite creature, humans—they were headed to extinction. She steeled herself for the spectacle—yet again—of human suffering.

• • •

Far from the sun, colonies of a single-celled organism were frozen, but not dead, on an asteroid. Momentum flicked some of the cells into space. A ship found them; the scientists aboard celebrated.

The demon was as ecstatic as the humans—they had discovered extraterrestrial life for the first time in this universe. Her happy moment ended. She knew what came next.

The cells were eukaryotic and capable of producing hexose from CO_2. The scientists hurried to save their greenhouse-gas suffocated world. After Nanopore and PacBio Sequel II genome sequencing, they found a gene cluster coding for a collection of proteins that promoted carbon sequestration, when expressed in yeast, by producing natural rubber from CO2. After more celebrating, they received a radio message from yet another alien lifeform: *There is intelligent life on other planets and we are on our way.*

The aliens showed up. They were herbivores, so there was no danger of direct predation, but there were always problems when humans discovered other sentients. Hybrid speciation occurred. Love between humans and aliens led to conflicts in politics, religion, and species self-identification. War ensued, then destruction.

The demon, from her vantage point atop the wall, saw this before it occurred. Knowledge boiled inside of her, begging—demanding—to be released. Despite loving humans, her nature compelled her to destroy universes she learned were headed for oblivion. Sadly, this was the fate of every universe she observed.

With one hand, she scooped up the universe, with the other, she lifted a sliding door on the wall's side, then threw the doomed universe in.

The wall didn't let her turn to see what was behind it, but she knew that nothing existed there, and once a universe entered, it was destroyed. The wall rumbled with contradiction, in enthalpic anger. The entropy lost in the destruction of the universe had to be repaid. Opening and closing the door on the wall resulted in a net zero energy consumption, but observing the defective universes required energy, heat, and entropy.

There was energy in information and information in memories. She made what looked like a *Che vuoi* gesture with both hands and forced her fingers into her eye sockets; they expanded like dislocated jaws. Her fingertips, now hotter than the sun, burned her memories. The wall consumed the heat and energy released from sizzling memories.

The past events were lost to her, but the echoes of suffering remained, like a blurry shadow with nothing to cast it.

Her instincts told her that she observed universes and destroyed them.

•　　•　　•

"I love you, Shannon," Henry said.

At that moment, Shannon—the demon—had accumulated enough memories in her human form to relearn what she actually was. She had been happy for a time, living a human life, as if the wall allowed her moments of ignorant respite between completing her duty.

The demon nearly frowned at Henry's declaration of love to her, but stopped herself. She couldn't remember the last time he'd said those words.

"I love you, too." It was true. She let a smile through. The amount of times she'd loved and lost were approximating infinite, yet she couldn't remember any specific details.

Henry coughed. Picoliters of blood spattered the machine monitoring his vitals. Peptide markers for lung cancer were solubilized in the blood. If she could remove the cancer from his body, sort the good cells from the bad, she would, but her power required physically touching the wall and was limited to universe observation, infiltration, and destruction.

"How much do you love me?" he asked.

Tears welled up in her eyes, her lips trembled. "I love you more than this universe."

He chuckled. The first time she'd said this, decades ago, he'd laughed and mansplained what clichés were. Now he found comfort in familiarity. The demon knew exactly how he felt, but not because she was omniscient. Her knowledge was far from infinite, but her power of observation was nearly so. She remembered the awkwardness of their first few dates, the first time they had sex, their daughter's high school graduation ...

"You always know everything," he said and winked at her. This was equal parts compliment and playful tease. "What do you think happens after we die?"

She bit the inside of her cheek and thought, *for me, I restart; for you, nothing.* "I think that your conscious self leaves your body and gets to travel through space, meet old friends, and have a lot of fun."

"Sounds more like what you hope happens," he said.

"It's both."

The demon looked out the hospital room's window, past the city's light pollution, past planets and galaxies.

There was a lifeform approaching this universe's Earth. It was multicellular, but simple and only achieved sentience transiently, when enough of the morula-like assemblies came together. Humans never figured out they had consciousness before the end, but learned that the blobs from outer space made novel cyclic peptides that treated a number of diseases. The demon rejoiced for a few milliseconds—her bliss immediately overwhelmed by the anticipation of pain and death.

After being harvested—and made to produce drugs against their will—for a few years, some assembled morula escaped and planned to eliminate humanity. They collaborated in a whole-genome duplication event, giving them enough redundant genes to mutate dozens of enzymes and produce volatile compounds that were toxic to humans. The humans never learned what sparked their extinction. She felt like she was choking alongside the future humans, until Henry spoke again.

"It makes me weirdly envious that everyone will keep living when I won't. Does that make sense?" Henry asked.

"You'll be alive in memories and thoughts," she said. "When you think about it, you probably spend most of your life in other people's thoughts. You think about Tricia every day, right?"

He smiled. "She's our only kid. Who else am I going to think about?"

"It's the same for me," the demon said. She got closer to Henry and squeezed his hand; it was cold and the grip weak. "But we only see her a few times a year. She spends more of her time in our thoughts and relived memories than in our physical presence. Death is just like that, except without the few meetings a year. You only lose the occasional interactions, really."

"What about the painful memories, and the fact that you'll never see that person again to form new memories? What if you hated everything they did?" he asked.

"I choose to only live in the good memories." This last part was a lie. The demon was not powerful enough to compartmentalize emotions. Pain seeped everywhere like radiation in the vacuum of space.

"I'm happy you're here," Henry said.

"I am too."

His face twisted in pain, but he recovered quickly. "Why did we ever get divorced?"

She shrugged and smiled. "I don't remember."

"Smartass," he said. Then he closed his eyes and fell asleep.

The demon sat up and rubbed her face. She looked at Henry and held back her tears. This pain would be his last. At this point, she had accumulated enough memories to burn and compensate for the destruction of this universe.

She deconstructed herself into macromolecules, then into atoms, then subatomic particles. Finally, she quantum tunneled to the wall instantaneously.

From this vantage, she saw the morula-assembling aliens flying through space in metal cylinders sent from another civilization attempting to xenomorph the Earth. She cursed at them.

She lifted the sliding door and tossed the universe that had made her a widow for the nth time—or so she assumed—through. The demon said, "My name was Shannon," and surveyed her past life like someone fast-forwarding through a movie. While burning her memories, she forgot the man's and young woman's names and why they were important. She was saddened from the emptiness left by lost memories, still knowing that she loved humans but not why, yet she was relieved of burden.

Then she forgot that she forgot.

•   •   •

Joan was so excited when she walked out of her physics lecture that she nearly had a spring to her step.

The professor had discussed a thought experiment called Maxwell's Demon, named after the famous physicist James Clerk Maxwell. In the experiment, a demon sat between two chambers, generically named A and B, both of which contained gas particles moving at different speeds. The demon's vision was so good that it could see single particles. There was a sliding door between the chambers that Maxwell's demon could lift, without applying work. After observing and waiting for a fast-moving particle from chamber A to approach, the demon would lift the sliding door and allow that particle to cross over to chamber B.

In contrast, the slow-moving particles from chamber B would get transferred to A. This resulted in chamber A cooling down and chamber B heating up instead of the temperature equilibrating between both chambers, seemingly violating the second law of thermodynamics.

It bothered Joan that the experiment felt so tidy, so contained. What were the chambers made of? Who made them? What was the point of it, anyways? She didn't know why she was obsessing about this all of a sudden, but felt some pride—obsessive behavior was lauded in the sciences.

"Hi babe, I'm home. I had a real galaxy brain moment because of class," Joan said as she walked into the apartment she shared with Phillip.

"We need to talk," Phillip said, sitting on the couch. The floor was littered with empty beer cans.

"It's a bit early to start drinking, right?" Joan asked. A sense of Déjà vu tickled her mind. Had she been here before? Dreamed this? Was this moment so generic that it felt familiar even though it had never happened?

"You know I love you, right? I mean I know you know," Phillip said. "Sorry, I drank a little. I'm just going to get to the point. I think we need some time apart. Maybe permanently."

"What?" Joan paced towards him, her stomach in knots. There were tears in her eyes already. "I love you more than anything. Our relationship is so good. We have so many things in common. What are the chances of finding that elsewhere?"

"I know." Phillip was jerking around now like a squirming worm, as if trying to kick start a motorcycle and flee. "I just want to meet other people. We're so young. You know? I don't know what I'm saying."

Joan screamed. "You want to leave just to fuck other women! I knew you were an asshole. And you had to get drunk to break up with me like an immature child. You think you're wasting time with me? It's me who's wasting time with a loser."

He stood, trembling fists at his side.

Joan was afraid but enraged.

As she pondered if he was capable of hitting her, she remembered what she was.

The wall. Destruction. Eternity.

Could she really love humans while hating the one in front of her? Was that hypocrisy or simply a statistical error?

"Ah, you reminded me of something," Joan—the demon—said. She was calm now. "I can't believe you're talking to me like I'm not enough for you when I am everything. You're just a little man I'll forget minutes from now."

"Wha—" Phillip looked at her with his face scrunched up in confusion.

"You reminded me of what I do. It saddens me to do it, but clearly sometimes I enjoy it. I prevent suffering by inflicting early pain and death. I know, a senseless system. But no one cares that I also hurt, and I also need to get stuff off my chest," the demon said, and transported herself back to the wall, unafraid Phillip was staring straight at her when she disappeared.

She picked up the universe she'd just left and heard Phillip scream cries of disbelief and madness. She was so angry she didn't investigate the havoc the alien ships travelling to Earth were going to do and simply destroyed the universe.

Her rage only increased now. How many times had she done this? Endless iterations of love and hate, or suffering and self-righteous anger. She stomped on the wall, trying to hurt it, but there was no result. She looked down from the wall. It was universes all the way down, but surely the wall must have a foundation somewhere. She tried to jump, but the wall held her feet in place; it was hungry for entropy.

She burned her memories to dissipate the rage and feed the wall. The anger lingered; it was impossible to carve out, like trying to scoop out tentacles of food coloring after it diffused in a glass of water.

She yanked her hair out to only see the amyloid fibrils depolymerize. Monomers sifted between her fingers.

The demon wept, until she had no idea why she was crying.

•   •   •

The yoga teacher, Maddy, was unique and funny enough for Max to fall in love with after only a few hangouts. She was a mathematician too—yoga and mathematics had made for an eye-catching combo on her Tinder profile.

"Max, girlie, we're going to be late," Maddy said, as she double-checked that her amateur telescope was ready for tonight's astronomy club meeting. "Get excited. What if we see a spaceship?"

Max sat on the bed, unmoving; she imagined that her own body was making a permanent impression into the mattress. "Something is bothering me."

Maddy sat beside her. "I get it. You're uncomfortable Kevin is going to be there, but there's nothing between us anymore. You know this."

Max shook her head. "I know, but it's something else."

Although, she was indeed jealous. How could something so small bother her so much? One could simply stop thinking about being jealous. She did the opposite and over-studied her feelings to find a way to get rid of them. The more she concentrated, the more abstract her feelings were, like squinting through myopic eyes to make sense of the fuzzy edges of an unknown shape.

She shrugged it off, and asked, "Do you think aliens actually exist? What are the chances?"

"I'm glad you asked. I'll tell you in the car," Maddy said.

Max looked out the passenger window to the stars and considered what kind of life could really be out there.

"The chances don't matter. As long as they are nonzero," Maddy said.

"What?" Max asked, confused. The stars brightened. They seemed to irradiate like cones of light. Max shook her head and cleaned her glasses.

"If the universe is infinite, then as long as the probability for life is nonzero then aliens *must* exist. And we're proof that life has a nonzero chance of existing. Infinity makes the impossible possible. I give my Calculus students an easy example." She went on. "First, you need to know that dividing by zero is nonsense. But if you knew a little bit more, you could instead approach zero and never get there."

After they parked, Maddy pulled out a napkin and pen from the glovebox and wrote:

$$\lim_{x \to 0} \frac{1}{x^2} = +\infty$$

"If *x* was zero then you're toast, but when *x* approaches zero, then the fraction approaches infinity," Maddy said. "There's life out there." She pointed to the sky.

"I just remembered…" Max said. She didn't need her glasses to see anymore. The stars were well-resolved dots with hard edges. She'd accumulated enough information to know what she was, which meant she could go back to the wall and never see Maddy again.

"What did you remember?" Maddy asked.

"Something I always forget before loving too much." Telling Maddy what she was would lead to confusion and disbelief. Why share negativity?

Maddy frowned, but didn't pry, probably to not risk opening a can of worms that would ruin the night.

"After we get back home, I'll remind you how flexible I am. How about that?" Maddy asked with an endearing wink.

"Can't wait," Max said. And she really meant it.

At the meeting, Maddy hugged Kevin; they giggled about something, then joined everyone else in setting up their telescopes. The jealousy left Max like dispersed mist. Only emotional numbness remained. After she destroyed this universe, so much love would be lost.

She took a turn on the telescope, not because she needed it to peer into space, but because why not pretend a little bit longer? Maddy's hand felt good on the small of her back.

This time, the travelers were mechanical, not water-based. The Skalart communicated with light. Atoms of different elements were compartmentalized in their bodies, and after being exposed to electromagnetic radiation, released photo-electrons of varying wavelengths. Humans quickly recognized this as the photoelectric effect, since the Skalart arrived on Earth many decades after Albert Einstein won the Nobel prize. Both sides were able to communicate well enough, but problems arose.

The Skalart's religion stated that they were the only beings in the universe able to communicate with any semblance of intelligence. Instead of updating their beliefs, they destroyed the Earth to force the universe into their divine teachings. They encountered other lifeforms and continued their cleansing until everything was destroyed.

The loss of life and gain in pain surpassed the amount of love produced by several orders of magnitude.

"Did you see anything you like?" Maddy asked when Max lifted her head from the telescope's eyepiece.

Max smiled, looking forward to the last time she'll have sex with the only person she'd loved in this life. "Nothing worth remembering."

•   •   •

Instead of destroying Maddy's universe, the demon sat on the wall, paralyzed with the fear of loss. She yelled at the wall, asking why she was burdened like this.

The wall was indeed alive in a sense; it consumed universes and demanded the release of entropy after all, but it never communicated back. The memories of how she began her task or details about her origin had been erased eons ago, or perhaps it had only been minutes.

The universes floated in front of the demon like little bubbles of anonymous nostalgia. She didn't have specific memories left over from the ones she'd destroyed, but there were emotional scars that were real yet alien, like the notion of dreams for a being that never slept.

She squinted and tried to find where the pool of universes ended, knowing the bubbles flocculated in suspension for infinity.

The wall didn't have an end either.

She thought of Maddy, of infinity, of possibilities.

In one of the universes in front of her, humans encountered another biological creature that also used antibodies in immune defense. The Dambamab could genetically engineer their bodies with their thoughts. After many decades, humans also developed technology to accomplish this. The biosciences lost much of their funding. *Why do research when we are gods of our bodies?* A Dambamab virus particle infected Earth. Most humans had opinions about what antibodies to produce. The loudest voices and conspiracies were followed, and humanity went extinct.

Before this happened, on a small island near Earth's equator, a woman in yoga pants bent over and touched her toes. The demon focused on the woman and felt a sense of longing.

She brought Maddy's universe up to eye level and saw that Maddy was crying. Maddy now spent most of her time stapling missing-person flyers with Max's face on them to telephone poles. The demon lifted the slot on the wall and felt relief from the anticipation, then closed it again. She couldn't destroy Maddy now—she would live, even if just for a little bit.

Part of the pent-up knowledge energy inside her diffused into Maddy's universe and it crystalized—the galaxies contorted into thermal ellipsoids. For the humans the changes were small, and it would take centuries for them to notice how weird space really had become—not that they would last that long.

She released the universe back into the pool. The urge to destroy and forget pulled at her like the gravity at an event horizon. She nearly snatched Maddy's home again, but instead she stood. Energy coated her legs like battery acid. She ran on the wall, searching.

There was no proof that all universes must end in destruction—there had to be a nonzero chance that humans and other creatures learned to live in harmony with each other. She'd find and learn from this outlier and force their model on other universes—maybe even in time to save Maddy. Perhaps there was even a way for her powers to be used in a constructive manner. Her lack of understanding of her own nature only opened possibilities.

Information converted into kinetic energy fueled the demon's legs as she ran. She repeated what Maddy had taught her, so she wouldn't forget: the remotely improbable became certainty, when approaching infinity.

MAGNETIZATION AND RESISTANCE

"No caigo en ese truco dos veces. Ese perro ya me mordió."
("I'm not falling for that trick twice. That dog already bit me.")
– Puerto Rican saying

THE ELEVATOR STOPPED on the second floor of the university's chemistry building, and Bárbara poked her head out to make sure the hallway was empty. The smell of antiseptic came from the labs, but there was no one around.

She hurried past the third lab to her right, where she'd conducted organic chemistry research for the last 30 years, steeling herself to avoid of thinking of the golden days of her work, before being fired. Instead, she filled the compartment where grief goes with hate for the robots.

The second-floor bathroom was also empty. She crouched under the sink, grabbed a vacuum-sealed plastic package hidden behind the plumbing, then slid it into her coat's inside pocket.

She'd been extra careful these past few days while moving wastebaskets with small amounts of used toilet paper from the bathrooms to the lab that had the vacuum sealer. She'd needed to collect nearly every wastebasket in the building since most people flushed their toilet paper. She got back in the elevator, pushed the button marked B, and told herself to not wimp out. If everything went well, her actions wouldn't hurt any real people.

The elevator ride gave her enough time to go over the last couple of months in her mind. Her stellar record at graduating students, generating innovative scientific ideas and years of work hadn't been enough to keep her researcher job away from the hands of a robot. Last year—thanks to the tenure revocation laws—Bárbara had been re-assigned to custodian duties until she retired, and despite her newly found permanent depression, tried to make the best of it. At least, she hadn't been fired and abandoned like so many other people in similar positions, but that kind of luck didn't strike the same place twice.

Her role in the university had changed, but her passion for teaching remained strong. No one cared if she helped students during her free time. Yet, remembering the meeting she had the week before made Bárbara's teeth clench in anger as she made her way through the building's basement.

Derrick Rhodes, the school's dean of Robotic and Automated Labor had given her his personal promise that the new robot would only take half her custodian shift for a short time, and that replacement was out of the question.

"After a couple of weeks, the robot will be evaluated. If it passes the test phase—which they always do—it'll be assigned elsewhere." Rhodes had even attempted to rationalize the situation by saying, "Why not let them do the jobs that they're better at than we are? I'd let them have my job if they had enough of the human touch required to do it."

Somehow Bárbara had doubted he'd give his job away so easily—never mind the fact that it was inane to think that an administrator needed a human touch to do his job—but she had other problems. Not only did a robot steal her previous job, but its scientific output was also outstanding. Objectively, a future when artificial intelligence evolved beyond human understanding was unavoidable. Still, the void left after losing her lab felt like she'd been dismissed from human productivity.

She checked her phone. It was nearly 6 am. The robot custodian's shift had finished almost half an hour before. She made her way to the lab in the basement to find the usual pristine scene the robot left behind. The floor was immaculately clean, chairs and tables polished so carefully they could be thought of as new—the robot's efforts were worthy of envy to anyone who cared. Bárbara cared. She didn't stand a chance. It had even scraped the pieces of chewing gum from under the tables. Hopefully, the gum would find its way into his cogs and give him a mechanical stroke.

She walked around the room, reconsidering her plan. Perhaps sabotaging the robots and having them removed wasn't the strongest approach, but for now it was the only idea she had. She only needed to be employed a few more years before being able to retire, anyway.

A white cylinder, ten feet tall and seven feet wide, occupied the center of the basement. Inside, magnetic slabs surrounded a solenoid micro coil. Orange traffic cones sat on the floor, forming a circular perimeter around the cylinder, indicating how far the magnetic field reached. Red tape ran along the floor, below where the cones should go, in case they were moved by accident. Erased credit cards were the most common victims for students who forgot to empty their pockets before approaching the magnet. This technology had applications ranging from drug discovery to MRI. A few more scientific instruments sat in the chemistry department's basement, but nuclear magnetic resonance spectroscopy, NMR, was Bárbara's expertise, and this NMR instrument was like her baby.

Two of her previous students had complained about issues with the NMR's software, and the thought of fixing it had kept her up the night before. Despite being in a hurry, Bárbara sat in front of the computer linked to the NMR and spent a couple of minutes debugging the system by updating lines of computer code. After finishing, she was certain that the computer would obey her absolutely.

Immediately after, she opened the vacuum-sealed package she'd hid in the bathroom and removed some of the contents with a pair of tongs. Used toilet paper hung like poisonous tentacles.

The stench reminded her of a gas station bathroom. With an outstretched arm, she wiped the countertops until the stink became overwhelming, then threw the paper in the wastebasket by the front door. She turned the lights off and fast walked to the parking lot like a saboteur who'd left a ticking bomb behind. No doubt the mess would be cleaned up as soon as it was reported, but hopefully enough PR damage would be done.

In the parking lot, a metallic clanking came from behind her after she opened her car door. She turned to see a robot standing with palms resting over what looked like a third trimester pregnancy belly. The bulbous, distended midsection was designed to store tools. The engineers claimed this way the robot's hands were free from having to carry baggage, efficient. Aesthetically, the designers also claimed that male looking robots with pregnancy bellies made them look more trustworthy.

"Hello, my name is John John," the robot said, then raised one of its hands to wave before letting it fall on its belly with a clunk.

The robot leaned forward, pivoting on its waist, as if its feet were glued to the floor. Plastic, unfocused eyes stared at Bárbara. A pale, waxy material served as the robot's skin.

John John wore a blue jumpsuit with a circular hole in the middle to accommodate the robot's midsection; its eyelids clicked with each blink.

The robot read her name tag. "You're Bárbara Morales. What a nice coincidence. I just finished my duties and have been waiting for the bus for 20 minutes, but it's great to meet you. I thought today was your day off. I am the new sentient unit delivered to split the night shift with you. I am sure you have many questions, but don't worry, I am not here to replace you, only to help. I am also well versed in human psychology and can serve as a friend, and we can discuss any frustrations you have." John John straightened, waited, then continued babbling. "I am also shy. I know transitions are hard, yet I am sure ours will be easier. Dean Rhodes informed me you were from Puerto Rico," the robot winked, "I know you have already adapted from life in another country, even another language. Fortunately, you only need enough English to get by. No one judges people by their accents. In fact, I'm not even a person," John John laughed while moving his head from side to side like an inverted pendulum, "making my situation worse than yours."

Bárbara opened her mouth, nearly reciting every swear word she knew in both English and Spanish but thought better of it. An outburst of anger would only arouse suspicion.

"So, what do you say, Bárbara Morales. Can we be colleagues? And keep this place clean and the research and teaching ongoing for many years to come?"

Bárbara exhaled a long breath and unclenched her stomach, smiled, then said, "No hablo Inglés." She got in her car and drove off.

•　　•　　•

She came in half an hour before her shift started on the next afternoon. Only the two undergraduate students she often helped with classes occupied the basement. No emails describing an unexplainable reek of urine had been sent. An administrator somewhere had to be keeping it quiet.

One of the students stood in front of the chemical fume hood. The other sat near the computer, swiping through her phone.

"What sample are you preparing?" Bárbara asked.

Michael, the student working in the fume hood, turned. "Just a quick test sample to make sure the tube is clean." He handled the thin, straw-like NMR tube deftly, preventing any damage to the clear borosilicate glass.

Lisa, still looking at her phone said, "Hi, Dr. Morales."

"Hi."

Bárbara let a few moments pass. "Do you guys know if anything happened here today?"

They shook their heads, seemingly without giving the question a second thought.

Nothing she could do then. "Put your phone away so we can start." Bárbara waited for Michael to walk over, and until the phones and wallets were in a basket by the table. In addition to credit cards, any electronics could be damaged if too close to the magnet. She entered a command in the computer and told Michael, "Go put the sample in."

"I'm still glad you take out of your time to teach us, Dr. Morales, especially when you don't have to. The robots are like mobile audiobooks. I don't learn anything in class. It's awful," Lisa said.

Robots "taught" by reading textbooks out loud in a non-inflected, accent-free voice, eliminating stylistic differences that led humans to be labeled as good or bad teachers.

Now, all teachers were equal.

Exorbitant increases in tuition rates had allowed the school to swap cheap adjunct professors for objective machines. Many supporters claimed that robot instructors improved teaching to the same extent that a calculator was better than an abacus.

"Let me see what you need to do for class," Bárbara said to Lisa, who passed her a notebook opened near the middle. A slew of differential equations, complex diagrams, and instructions covered the page. Turning the page, Bárbara found more math that she recognized as a formalized theory justifying why NMR worked, how similar it was to an MRI done in a hospital setting, alongside more drawings of nuclei spin systems flipping in and out of Boltzmann distributions.

"I'm guessing this is gibberish to you," Bárbara said.

"The robot is reading the first few chapters of an advanced physics book in class. But I'm pre-med and haven't taken calculus yet," Michael said.

This is like teaching someone how to read by giving them a dictionary, Bárbara thought.

"My parents are forcing me to stay in school, because they think that as long as I do my best, I'll be okay. They like to emphasize that doctors aren't being replaced," Michael said. "But we all know the truth. Doctors aren't being replaced *yet*."

Bárbara nodded. The rationale behind what jobs were given to robots eluded everyone except the policy makers in charge. Priests and politicians were off-limits since these required "an irrational and loving human heart", yet teachers, service industry workers, and scientists had been deemed obvious choices since their duties were thought to be easily automated. Universal basic income was also being discussed, but unlike passing laws that allowed robots to replace people in their jobs—despite in-place protections such as tenure professorship—deciding how much and when to pay the displaced workers was "the trickiest economic problem of our times" and hence no legislation had been passed.

"You're driving the NMR today, Lisa," Bárbara said.

Lisa wrote the commands Bárbara told her and hit go. Instead of one signal for chloroform, the computer screen was sprinkled with thin peaks.

"What's this?" Michael asked.

Lisa shook her head. "Garbage. You contaminated it."

"No. I didn't," Michael said, then shook his head rapidly, as if shedding away the possibility that he made a mistake. "I cleaned everything as best as I could."

Bárbara stood and walked to the fume hood. "Come here for a minute." When both students walked over, she pointed to a warped plastic pipette beside the chloroform bottle. "It's melted."

Michael let out a frustrated sigh. Lisa rolled her eyes.

"I forgot. Plastic dissolves in chloroform," Michael said.

"It happens to everybody; don't worry. Find a new bottle and make it again." Bárbara said.

The door opened and she saw her supervisor, Adrián, shyly signal her over.

"Bárbara, can we talk?" he asked, fumbling his fingers in front of his chest. She made the most innocent-looking expression she could muster, told the students to continue on their own, and followed Adrián outside.

"Something happened this morning or last night. I don't know," he said.

Here it comes, she thought. "What?" she asked with a straight face.

"Well ..."

"Adrián que pasó—"

He put his hand up. "It's better if we stick to English while on campus. Some professors get irritated when we speak Spanish."

Bárbara sighed, forcing several comments addressing Adrián's lack of character to the back of her mind. "Okay."

Adrián pulled her away from the door and spoke in a quiet voice. "This morning, I found toilet paper in that room's trash can."

Bárbara pointed behind her shoulder with her thumb. "Where? In here. I've never seen people cleaning the lab glassware with toilet paper, but maybe it leaves less scratches. Who knows?" She shrugged.

Adrián frowned, and his lips curved downward as if gravity was pulling them off his face. "It was used. And an awful smell everywhere. Luckily, I doused everything in bleach hours before anyone walked in."

Bárbara cupped her hand over her mouth, unable to decide if her performance was award-winning quality or over the top. "That's horrible. It might be the anti-robot protesters. They probably caught on that one has been assigned with us. They do all sorts of vandalism." She paused for a few seconds, wanting to push Adrian's thinking in the right direction without being too obvious. "On the other hand, how does the robot clean? Does it keep all the trash in its belly and move from place to place? Maybe it forgot. You know, they can't smell the same way we do. Sure, they can detect volatiles in the parts per billion range but who knows."

"I'm told the chance that the robot made a mistake is very low. If one of the professors that opposes robot workers finds out, it would start some serious gossip."

"Maybe it's for the best. If they can't do the job, then that's that."

"No, Bárbara. The best is to keep our heads down and follow the rules." His face reddened, but he continued in a whisper. "Did you have anything to do with this? This is one of the robot's first few shifts shared with you. This could look bad on all of us. I'm your supervisor and I wouldn't want to be associated with —"

Bárbara raised her hand. She felt betrayed. "I'd appreciate that you don't spread rumors and lies if you don't have any proof. I have a family too and need this job as much as you do. And don't worry, your English is better than mine and you're whiter than me. We won't be lumped together."

"That's not what I meant." After a moment, Adrián spoke. "Let's keep this between us for now. Rhodes knows of course. He told me he'd take care of it."

"Okay. I need to clock in. Excuse me." Bárbara walked away. She didn't smile and giggle until she reached the restroom and made sure she was alone. The wastebaskets in the stalls had a few pieces of paper again. After a couple of days of collecting more paper, she could repeat her plan. If she made John John look like an incompetent nitwit repeatedly, he'd surely get decommissioned. Next time, she'd make sure someone apart from Adrián found her work first.

•   •   •

The next day, Bárbara listened to music on her phone while cleaning. Her shift flew by before she knew it as she sang along with one of her favorite Salsa songs, *Todo tiene su final, nada dura para siempre...* All things end, nothing lasts forever.

She stopped singing when John John walked in. Another robot, with the same plastic-white, pasty face followed.

"Hi Bárbara. This is Mike," John John said.

"Mike Mike?" Bárbara asked, smiling.

"No. Just Mike." The other robot said.

"I know. It's a joke."

Both robots looked at each other, then turned back to her, and tilted their heads from left to right while cackling.

"Mike is our new supervisor," John John said after they quieted down.

"What about Adrián?" Bárbara's smile disappeared.

"He was let go," Mike said. Both robots lowered their heads as if taking a moment of silence for the recently deceased.

Confusion mixed with anger grabbed at her throat. "What? Why did—"

"Bárbara, I know you're upset. Let me explain." Mike inhaled and sighed, despite having no need for oxygen. "Usually, humans in supervisory positions are not eligible for labor substitution, but it's better for our learning experience if we remain with those who are the same as us. We are more comfortable. We learn from our experiences but also from each other. It's exponentially better this way. Of course, the goal is to approach being more human, which I hope to achieve after supervising you."

Bárbara hid her trembling fists behind her back. She nearly asked if they knew what irony was. Intense pressure pounded on her temples and she squeezed her eyes shut.

"Are you okay? Women of your age are at an increased risk of heart-related incidents. Before coming here, my programmer said that it is better to ignore things one cannot change," Mike said.

"I'm fine," Bárbara said through trembling lips.

Mike nodded and turned to John John, unlatching the lid on top of John John's belly. Screwdrivers and wrenches clinked against metal as he pulled them out.

"Are you guys handy*men* now too?" she yelled.

Both robots laughed.

"We are practicing hand-eye coordination. Every model is different. I'll email you a set of tasks aimed at optimizing your productivity. Especially—" Mike continued talking as Bárbara stormed out of the room.

Bárbara cried as she slammed her fist against her car's steering wheel. The robots would eventually take all the jobs, and she'd done her best to keep her own. Getting Adrián fired in the process wasn't her intention. If only the robots hadn't been slowly taking her job away a second time, none of this would've happened. Sending Mike after John John had "fucked up" was the stupidest approach towards solving the problem, like overlaying two Band-Aids over a deep gushing wound. She wiped her tears with the back of her hand and took a few deep breaths. Guilt gripped her chest like a vise. Adrián's persistence to not speak Spanish in public was only one aspect of his personality she detested. Yet, he didn't deserve to get fired and have his family suffer, much less for actions he didn't commit.

In other industries, such as truck driving and fast-food restaurants, robots had taken over nearly every job, and no number of protests—violent or otherwise—had led to change. A lucky few had received nice pensions or were in situations like

Bárbara, but for the most part, people were fired without a second thought.

The next step in labor substitutions had had a larger financial aim. Every news outlet summarized it with the same question: Could robots outthink humans in conducting medical research and save billions of dollars in the process? And the truth was that the robot that had replaced her was publishing papers left and right since it never slept.

If she wanted to keep her job, and maybe get Adrián re-hired, she needed to increase the aggression. Making the robots look like idiots was too soft a goal. She needed to hit the system where it really hurt.

After getting home, she calculated the decay of a magnetic field. Magnetic field strength had an inverse cube relationship with distance. The calculation was easy, but she still double checked it. She tried to sleep, waiting until the robot shift ended, then returned to the chemistry department's basement. She made sure to leave all metal items, her purse, and phone by the computer. The silence in the room told her there was no one around. The joints in her hands and knees ached as she stripped the red tape from the floor, and made a new perimeter closer to the NMR, then she set the cones on top of the new tape line.

• • •

Bárbara walked into the basement and dropped the spray bottle, spilling blue glass cleaner on the floor.

"Oh my God," she said, forcing tears down her cheeks; definitely award-winning acting.

Stuck to the magnet were John John and Mike. The robot bodies were twisted into each other like a pair of contortionists that had attempted a two-human pretzel.

"I don't know how this happened," the chemistry department chair, Dr. Markson, said. "They had been warned many times. No metal beyond the cones."

Bárbara tensed for a second, but neither of them men noticed that someone had moved the perimeter a bit closer to the NMR. Her trap was too subtle for these two bureaucrats to pick up on.

Director Rhodes nodded. "This is not good. A good number of students came in before we closed off the floor. I'm guessing the noise made them curious. It's all over social media already. Why are their faces melted like that?" He looked over to Bárbara, but she continued to cry, covering her mouth in case a smile slipped.

"A bottle of some organic solvent must have made its way over and probably shattered when they smashed into the magnet, spilling the liquid everywhere. Maybe one of them was holding it while the other cleaned," Dr. Markson said, pointing to broken glass beneath one of the robot's hanging feet. "This is going to be unimaginably expensive to fix."

"If a student had been here and ended up hurt, we'd be on our way to court already," Rhodes said.

That was all she needed to hear. Bárbara turned to leave and surreptitiously took a picture of the two deformed robots from the door.

Once she got home, she made a meme with the picture side by side a Freddy Kruger snapshot, the main bad guy from the movie *A Nightmare on Elm Street*, then captioned her meme with "Who wore it better?" She posted the meme on a fake twitter account and tagged the school, the chemistry department, even Rhodes' personal account. Enough students were talking about it online, so no one would suspect her.

That evening, her phone pinged with an email. It was long, and full of official language stating that robots had been banned from campus until future notice. She was sure they would be back soon enough though. Many jobs depended on them.

Some science departments were concerned about how much safety awareness robots had, especially those that mentored students in a lab setting. If the robots were immune to most toxic substances, could they still have enough empathy to protect human students when around said substances?

A file was also attached to the email, a job offer, giving Bárbara a non-tenure track professor and researcher position, along with a significant amount of money from the chemistry departments' emergency fund to restart her lab. New challenges might arise in the few years before she retired, but those were problems she'd address as they arrived. She accepted the offer immediately.

REGRET IN BLUE SHARP

D R. MARKSON CRANKED his lantern on, then searched the argillaceous, rocky wall for a smooth patch. The light glimmered against crystalline minerals coating the cavern's stalactites. He became short of breath and bent over, then straightened up slowly, keeping the light on the wall and standing still until his respiration rate returned to normal. Spots appeared in his vision, but he managed to dispel them by blinking rapidly, like the trill of a flute. Fatigue was catching up to him, but luckily, Cassandra's orchestra couldn't be much further into the tunnels.

He found a dry spot on the wall, a few feet before the tunnel forked into two, and drew an arrow pointing to where he'd come from with his chalk.

As a young man, he'd challenge himself to memorize the endless turns of new caverns he surveyed. Unrelenting efforts, natural talent, and a sober mind had led his mentors to label him a student prodigy, a born critical thinker, an exemplary scientist, feeding his ego at a moment in time when he believed that personal happiness and self-identity necessitated professional success. But now Markson was old, and the accumulating grief of the last few decades had stripped away many of his cognitive abilities, like water patiently washing away stubborn stone. He was also old enough to know others wouldn't understand what he needed to do. So, he had come to this cavern alone, searching for the source of the music. Soon he'd be deep enough to hear the melody clearly, and Cassandra would be waiting at the source.

It had taken months to chase the source of the music to this cavern. Months of waking dreams, and puzzling together cryptic melodies, indicated only one outcome. Cassandra was here. It didn't make sense how he knew this, but it was a certainty. It wasn't necessarily logical that both of his loves, cave systems and Cassandra, had intertwined in one place. Perhaps it was fate.

At first, he'd thought the orchestra was a symptom of his deteriorating mental health, only to later realize that it was a summoning—Cassandra clamoring for his presence. He tried explaining to his friends the voice was unambiguously hers, but they had insisted he see a mental health specialist. Eventually, he gave in and visited a doctor, and took his medication for a whole month but never refilled the prescription. For a time, her voice had stopped—

"I am waiting, my love," Cassandra's voice interrupted his thoughts, re-establishing her existence. She continued speaking, but in a gradual decrescendo until he only heard the susurration of unintelligible whispers. Which words she spoke didn't matter. They were surely a declaration of love.

A squeak like a clarinet with a split reed came from his right, and he decided to follow that path, ignoring the arthritic grind in his knees and ankles as he walked. At the tunnel's threshold, the ground became uneven, and he lowered the lantern to see where his feet landed.

Scattered puddles of water emulsified with organic oils shone with iridescence, creating what looked like a warped rainbow disjointed across the ground. He did his best to avoid slipping on the puddles. No one knew he was here, so if he injured himself, help wouldn't come.

But he only needed Cassandra. She would take him back after seeing how much regret he felt and how hard he was trying to fix his mistakes, most of which were drowned in alcohol, inaccessible, or simply erased from his mind. His current journey in this cavern was evidence enough of his willingness. Who else would risk their lives in search of a past love? Isn't disregard for personal safety a sign of true commitment?

After getting back together, they could move back to a new city, start a new life. He could show off the few bits of music theory he'd studied and impress her. Maybe later she could re-join an orchestra and he could sit in the front row, heart swollen with pride as she played.

He breathed in the cool air and relaxed. Caverns comforted him like no other place, but they could be deadly without attacking. They instead waited, killing by combining a lack of resources with the victim's negligence, like a murderer with infinite time and patience, depriving their victims of food, water, and light, until their body and mind crumbled, then finally amalgamated with the mineral-rich earth. But he had enough experience to survive. During his career as a geologist, he'd spent long stretches of time studying new, unknown cave systems just like this one, then publishing his findings, moving up the academic ladder until he became head of his own department at the state university. His colleagues had nicknamed him Dr. Maze Hunter, an unoriginal attempt at mockery that didn't bother him. Eventually, he found out that some of his peers—the same that shared jokes and stories during cocktail hour—were preventing him from funding his lab by giving his grant applications poor evaluations. This betrayal angered him to no end, catalyzing drinking that led to violence that led to further drinking.

The sound of air rushing through a hollow object, like blowing into a trumpet with the mouthpiece missing, came from deep in the tunnel. He raised his lantern, but the light stopped several yards in front of him, as if blocked by a solid wall. He held his breath, strained his hearing, but there was only the sound of his colleagues laughing. He ground his teeth to stop himself from swearing back at them. The cackles made him punch the wall beside him, hurting his hand but at least banishing the voices. After a few minutes, he relaxed again, the pain in his hand the only reminder of what was no doubt a hallucinatory event—Cassandra wouldn't allow his enemies into this place.

The tunnel led to a large, cavernous chamber inundated with blue light. Bioluminescent animals glowed overhead, revealing the ceiling's rugged topography. The troglomorphic creatures had four legs and moved like nimble lizards. He'd never seen this species of reptile before. How deep into the cavern was he? He remembered traveling for a couple of days, yet the burlap sack he carried over his back was only half filled with bread and canned meat, so it must've been longer. He'd also re-filled the canteen hanging from his belt with the cavern's natural water sources countless times. Luckily, he'd spent long spans of time in caverns during his career and was able to keep his bearings.

After a few moments of consideration, he nicknamed the creatures blueups, since they were blue and came from above.

He walked deeper into the chamber, and a blue hue washed over his body. The hairs on his arms stood, as if reaching to an unseen source of static electricity. After taking a deep breath under the cool light, his mind quieted for several minutes.

Music started playing—softly, pianissimo—like a soothing lullaby. He spread his arms to take it in, to let the melody solvate into his blood like water-miscible alcohol, but the brasswinds lost the beat, rushing through the music, while the clarinets and flutes slowed down. The percussionists pounded against the snare drums like a drunk marching band. He plugged his index fingers in his ears. His stomach clenched with his staccato breath.

A familiar smell of gardenias and peonies came from his left.

"Do you know why I'm leaving?" Cassandra stood a few yards away, a violin case leaning on her side.

Warm gas ballooned in his throat. He burped and smelled the reek of partially metabolized bourbon despite the fact he'd been completely sober for weeks. The Cassandra in front of him wore the dress she'd donned in one of the few fights he remembered clearly. Luckily, the black eye he'd accidently given her had healed. He hadn't meant it, after all, but she had no right to suggest how to improve his career. He was the scientist, not her—no. That didn't sound right. Perhaps the fight had started for another reason.

"I am your wife, not your possession." She sighed. "It doesn't matter anymore. I've met other … I'm afraid of telling you." Cassandra raised her head, and tears ran down her cheeks.

"I tried. I failed. I'm sorry. Please come back." He took a few steps towards her.

"No! You'll never change." Cassandra slammed the case against the cavern's floor. "I won't waste my life giving you chances." She turned around to leave.

"Wait! I've changed. Please don't leave me again." He rushed to the image, hands outstretched, yearning to hug Cassandra and feel her soft skin. She dissipated before he reached her. The smell of her perfume lingered, and the cavern filled with laughter.

"No No No No No No!"

He rushed away from the blueups, running through tunnels and passages until the pain in his knees made him collapse, then realized the amateurish mistake of running directionless in this place. The hot anger in his heart had muted his rational mind. He needed music to avoid a panic attack, but the orchestra had gone silent. He sat upright and clapped at one hundred beats per minute. He'd practiced using a metronome and was confident he got the timing perfect. Every third clap he giggled to cheer himself up, keeping the pace of laughter near a grave tempo.

He eventually stopped clapping and prepared lunch while rationalizing how insensible it was to argue with hallucinations. Clearly, the real Cassandra intended he work a bit harder before finding her and wouldn't just appear and then disappear. Also, the real Cassandra left him without saying a word, bruises still visible.

His temples contracted and twitched, and pain dug into his skull. Despite not having had a single drink, he was experiencing the worst hangover he remembered. He laid on the cold ground. In the distance, he could almost hear her voice, whispering words of encouragement.

•   •   •

Some of the others already have partners. I know this because I have been nearly chosen several times, caressed by smooth flesh, even twirled on one occasion, yet no one has selected me for a permanent bond. I don't blame them. How hard would it be for me to choose a partner among such a vast selection of candidates? I cannot see or hear them, but I feel the vibrations they transmit, and in that hum, there is only happiness. Look at the eternal grins the partners wear if you don't believe me. Listen to the shrills of their ecstasy.

•   •   •

The pain in his right knee woke him. He stood from the floor and rubbed his leg, but the pain was deep in his joints, inaccessible to his fingers. He could have brought arthritis medication to relieve his symptoms, but coping with the stiffness and swelling on his own would show Cassandra how much he was willing to sacrifice for her, for them to be together again.

Some of his colleagues at the university regretted their old age, saddened that they wouldn't be able to continue their research. They'd spent their lives claiming they were close to the next great breakthrough. He pitied them.

Cassandra had been right: life was to be enjoyed without the need for outside validation of one's accomplishments.

He remembered when he'd shared with the other faculty that Cassandra was a musician, first violin in the city's orchestra. Most of his colleagues shrugged, unimpressed. He'd nodded and clinked whisky tumblers with them—a habit he'd developed on the job—thinking he, as a scientist, was objectively superior to an artist. After all, weren't artists simply entertainers of a sort?

"Not everything can be approached with scientific rationality," she'd said often. "Music is part of the irrational human truth."

He had laughed at her back then, but things changed. Even now he didn't know what she'd meant, but hints were starting to resonate within him.

A decade after she left, his scientific career was dead. One of his colleagues in a similar situation had found solace only in suicide. But Dr. Markson had found peace in art, partly because of the happy memories shared with Cassandra. Art was a form of beauty, a way to share one's most raw emotions. If science observed the physical world as it was, art created new things that need not exist, but that made life richer.

The orchestra played in the distance. He closed his eyes and tried to pick out the saxophone—his favorite instrument—but the sound was missing. Then, there was silence. Cassandra had told him the saxophone was not commonly played in orchestra, but she'd surely include one for him in the cavern's orchestra as a reward for trekking this long journey.

He bent his right knee several times, while leaning against the wall to avoid resting his entire weight on his left leg. Moving around helped with the arthritis. He continued, following the sound of running water, until he reached an underground river. Water dripped from the darkness above him. A naturally made stone bridge crossed over the river. The bridge's rocky surface helped his boots maintain purchase while he crossed. He heard the blare of a horn over what sounded like a person humming. His heart raced, as if telling him that he should be nervous and anxious, terrified even, yet he felt at ease, as if his body and mind were out of sync and couldn't agree on what to feel. When he reached the other side, he sat on the edge of the water with legs outstretched and refilled his canteen, then drank heavily until his heartbeat returned to a normal pace. He walked a few steps away from the water, pondered on the turns he'd taken after the panicked episode in the blueup's chamber, and drew an arrow on the floor.

·　　·　　·

Time cannot be measured here, only progress. I've learned how to move without damaging myself. My body remains untarnished. Our bodies will fuse together into one being, perfect in every way. Perhaps the end will finally come.

·　　·　　·

His food supply had run out long ago, and he decided to risk his health by eating the blueups. The gelatinous fluid inside their bellies tasted acidic and reminded him of times he'd vomited after drinking too much, yet they served to keep the hunger away. His beard had become long enough to catch some of the half-chewed morsels when they wriggled out of his mouth. The hand crank on his lantern had broken off, and he'd filled the alembic-shaped glass chimney with the blueups, which in addition to lighting his way also gave him a perfect place to store his food.

His mind was getting better. The hallucinations only began when he thought about them. "I'm not thinking of you," he said. "I made mistakes, but I've repented. The silence here is beautiful."

He sang snippets of his favorite songs to distract himself. Vocalizing Frank Sinatra's "My Way" eventually calmed him. It had been some time since he'd heard his own voice. His intonation was better than he remembered. Why hadn't it ever occurred to him that he could be a singer?

•   •   •

He is close. The air vibrates with excitement. Is he calling out to me? I'll tap my neck against the hollow wooden floor until we're together. It is true this is a trap. It is also providence.

•   •   •

Dr. Markson's beard stretched down to his waist like wet, gray tendrils. The tunnel continued to spiral down around him. The supply of blueups was endless. They provided a hint of accomplishment if he ate enough, like quitting a night of drinking after only three beers. He'd accepted this place as his new home, his chalk crushed and abandoned on some anonymous rock. The hallucinations no longer bedeviled him.

He grabbed a handful of blueups and chewed on them several dozen times, until the noodle-like creatures became a viscous mush in his mouth. If he swallowed them whole, they gnawed at his throat and stomach, peppering his stomach lining with bloody ulcers, a fact he only knew because of the blood he'd coughed up. Indeed, swallowing them like jello shots had not been a good idea.

The ground became crystal white and sloped down. He immediately recognized the salt as potassium sodium tartrate, a piezoelectric material that when deformed by mechanical stress produced electrical charge, his favorite organic salt.

"What a coincidence," he said and clapped his hands with joy—this time at 120 beats per minute, a consistent allegretto.

He made his way down the salt slope, resting his palm against the wall to keep his balance. The ground beneath his feet vibrated with every step, and the hairs on his nape stood.

The rapping sound he'd been following for months, or perhaps even years, became a single word inside his mind.

Love. Love. Love.

Uncontrollable lust goaded him down the slope. Part of his mind screamed that he was being lured into oblivion, like an insect voluntarily treading to the heart of a spider's web, hopelessly seduced, unable to turn and flee.

He continued walking, turned left. A red curtain hung at the end of his path. Tartrate salt coated the folds like powdered sugar on a pastry. When he touched the curtain, electricity crackled up from the ground to the ceiling. Slowly, the curtain moved to the side, revealing a wooden stage covered with rows of metal chairs. In each chair sat an immobile skeleton holding a musical instrument. Farthest from him, the skeleton conductor stood, its left hand over its head, clutching the baton. Beyond the conductor were rows of red plush chairs filling a massive theater.

His hand trembled as he ran his fingers over the clavicle of the skeleton manning a timpani, streaking white powder off the bones.

Lying on the floor, behind the skeletons holding flutes up to their lipless mouths, a saxophone bumped its neck against the floor repeatedly at 60 beats per minute, like a clock. He waited until the instrument stopped moving, but it continued, swaying and tapping against the floor in perpetual motion, unaware that this mere action violated the first law of thermodynamics. Here, in this place that ignored the constraints of known physics, he'd found the orchestra. Cassandra had to be close.

He walked over, careful not to disturb the immobile musicians, and picked up the saxophone. After touching the cool metal, a voice spoke in his mind. "I loved you, but you failed me."

His voice trembled. "Cassandra?"

The saxophone continued. "I'm so tired of the rotations and the cycles of violence. Periodicity governing over delicious chaos."

He held his breath, expecting yet another hallucination to pass and Cassandra to appear from the darkness and hold him in her arms.

"I am real. Stop thinking and feel me. I am sad for you. I'm sick of talking to you after you've lost your mind. Every time, the same thing." Cassandra sighed. "You can't apologize for a life of mistakes, but don't worry. This is the last iteration. The end of the end of everything."

The only seat unoccupied by a skeleton was the one in front of the saxophone. What felt like cold fingers grabbed the back of his head, while another force, accompanied by the sound of someone blowing out a candle, shut his eyes and brought the instrument up to his face. The mouthpiece felt natural in his mouth, the reed rough against his tongue. He blew without wanting to, and the saxophone told him that sound was called G, and that he was perfectly tuned.

He straightened his spine. The arthritic pain in his lower back felt like he'd been stabbed with a red-hot chimney rod. His hands released the saxophone, but it floated in place, forcing him to blow again. This time the orchestra tuned with him.

He opened his eyes and saw that every skeleton had been replaced with a replica of himself. The flute players were the youngest, while the percussionists in the back were the oldest. The haircuts, weight, and general facial features varied, but they were all him, a Markson orchestra. Fear made his face twitch, his legs tremble, he needed to urinate, but the saxophone forced him still.

An orchestra of failure, Cassandra's voice told him.

Instead of a skeleton, Cassandra—not the one he'd loved, but a nearly identical twin—now conducted the orchestra. Her gaze locked with his, and he winced like an injured animal. He wished he had his medicine, a vanishingly small organic molecule capable of hushing the music and stopping the visions, leaving real peace behind, but taking a pill wouldn't help. His surroundings felt too real to be hallucinations.

Beside his own reflection on the saxophone's polished bell, Cassandra stared back. He looked around. On every instrument he could see, her face smiled at the other versions of him.

Was he looking at previous versions of himself? Was his society another in a line of infinite repetitions? Had human history replayed itself; forced onto a deterministic cycle of being born, growing old, and dying?

In front of him lay a phenomenon unknown to science. A collection of questions that if published would lead to a long string of high-tier publications and abundant grant money, a clear direction for his research career during his next life.

But her voice had been clear. There was no next time.

He needed to escape. He needed to find happiness. Still holding the saxophone, he'd turned to the curtains when the sound of cracking glass came from above him. A diamond shaped salt formation protruded from the ceiling. A blue, viscous liquid sloshed within, writhing unto itself like semi-solid hydrophobic tubes. The diamond cracked again, and fist-sized salt crystals fell around him.

He tried to run, but the saxophone ordered him to stop. The pain in his joints flared, and against his will, he stopped moving. The crystallized salt shattered. A giant mass of blueups cascaded down and piled on the floor. A blue wave of electricity hit his right side just below the ribcage, shocking his liver, and after a few moments of intolerable pain, he smelled burning flesh; his heart beating past prestissimo.

"It is a bad thing to die in pain and confusion," Cassandra said.

Cassandra's voice came in bellows, a projection that resonated in all of reality. He had nearly grasped the meaning of her words when a flurry of images showed him the abominable deeds he'd done while intoxicated and had later forgotten—violence in drunk stupors with hints of a sense of superiority, self-exculpation...pleasure. He knew what he was: an unimportant, small man that didn't deserve forgiveness, whose own name disintegrated into the air like burning ash. The anonymous man took a deep breath, welcoming the electrifying pain. Then darkness extinguished his thoughts.

•   •   •

We are finally complete. The mistress stands straight, clicking her stick against the music stand and signaling us to start playing. Even if you're sane, the braces imprisoning your mind will fall apart, elevating your senses.

Don't fret if you hear our music calling. The pain will be short.

All cycles have been completed. If you hurry, you'll catch my solo. It will make your hearts burst with love. My husbands will play while you soak in the blood and sweat of your efforts, the last orgy of men.

When the last note is played, and the last instrument crumbles to dust, we'll fall from this plane, plummeting through unknown dimensions, regrets intact and inerasable.

BIG WATER
PROTECT YOU

I COULDN'T SEE THEM HIDING in the thick vegetation covering El Yunque—Puerto Rico's tropical rain forest—but the moans of the dead came loud and clear, accompanied by the squelching of wet soil beneath my boots, following me through the forest like a slow-moving orgy ascendant from hell.

We were supposed to have landed near a defensible position, but after clearing the Caribbean Sea, our poorly maintained aircraft decided to take a nosedive into the Earth. Only I'd survived—a fact I was still deciding how I felt about. After navigating the gore of my brothers and sisters in arms, I headed west. Why? Because my home was that way. Who knows, maybe one of my childhood neighbors had survived this man-made apocalypse and spent their days watching the dead shamble up and down the street, while sipping their morning coffee.

This made me officially AWOL. If I still had the means to fight, and the enemy still stood, I was to sit tight and wait for the next patrol, but seriously, *fuck* the Army. My loyalty was valued at a one-to-one exchange. You only get back what you put in; they hadn't put in enough for me to sit here and die.

Two naked tangos appeared from beside a grouping of bent ferns, dragging their feet like they were made of lead. I raised my rifle and dropped both, one shot to the head each. I had ten rounds left. If I didn't find a way out, or at least a place to hunker down, I'd end up as a fully organic lunch, at best early dinner.

I crossed a clearing covered in mud. Water seeped through my so-called waterproof combat boots, yet another lie from the Empire.

The sounds of running water drowned out the sounds of the dead. After a few minutes, I reached a wooden bridge crossing over a rushing river. I froze in place when I saw a group swaying and slow dancing in a loose circle around several ripped drums, leathery flesh wrapped around bones like dried jerky. My heart beat against my ribs like a prisoner punching iron cell bars.

The dead opened and closed their mouths, releasing moans in what sounded like deliberate chants. Some wore loincloths. Stringed seashells hung around the necks of the women. The scene resembled an Areyto, a traditional dance of the Taíno people who populated the island before being enslaved, raped, and eradicated by Spanish colonizers five hundred years ago.

I knelt, resting my rifle against my shoulder, forcing my hands to stop trembling. Part of me wanted to eliminate the zombie threat, while another felt disgusted at lifting arms against my ancestors.

This complication told me the problem was worse than we thought. The exact mechanism causing the dead to rise remained unknown, but the tie to the CRISPR/Cas9 technology was undeniable. This advancement in molecular biology had helped cure many diseases, but the enzymological cocktail used in many treatments, infused with DNA replication and RNA translation machinery, animated the recent—and not so recent—

dead. Yet, DNA degraded over time. How could these bodies be reanimated after being dead for so long? Despite the threat standing in front of me, the scientist in me found a few seconds to formulate a hypothesis. I remembered a lecture I'd attended at Harvard many years ago. The speaker showed a picture of a human skull, and with glee recounted how she'd coincidentally discovered that the inner ear was a perfect storage place for DNA, keeping the biomolecule stable for thousands of years.

One of the Taínos turned its head, empty eye sockets leveled with my gaze. Spooked, I squeezed the trigger. The bullet hit its right shoulder. A dead Taíno woman bit into the gunshot wound, then spat the bullet towards me. It clinked on the wooden bridge. Cold sweat ran down my nape. The woman set foot on the bridge. Another male walked into the river, sinking like a stone. I wasn't naïve enough to think he'd drown or get pulled downstream.

I opened fire, aiming for their brains. Puffs of brown powder exploded from behind their heads. My gun ran out of bullets before all the bodies dropped. I saw the silhouette of a person in the water, walking on the river's bottom. I ran, racing parallel to the rushing water.

Confusion and fear swam in my mind as blood pounded against my temples. That the ancient dead could be revived was one thing, but biting a bullet out of a wound… Signs of intelligence were a whole new problem.

Obtaining a Ph.D. in biochemistry hadn't kept me from being drafted by the U.S. Army. Even worse, instead of a cushy job in a lab somewhere, they'd sent me back home to help solve The Plague, a catastrophe of their own making. What could I do? I was an expert in biocatalysts, but none of this made sense to me.

Surely, I'd be promoted from lieutenant cannon fodder to captain expendable meat if I went back and reported what I'd found. But that wasn't in my plans. They'd figure it out eventually. Rumors were that some pharmaceutical companies had dumped their waste near Native American gravesites; it was out of sight and vastly cheaper. Those executives better hope they were as good at dodging the dead as they were at evading taxes.

I stopped and leaned against a tree, coughing phlegm. The green canopy above me blocked the sun. Was I still running westward?

I couldn't believe it. I was going to die, dehydrated, and lost in my own home. I should've stayed here. What did I gain by leaving, anyway? I had a better shot at the American Dream by lying down here and falling asleep. I looked at the sky, imagining everything I'd do differently if I had another chance. One thing was for certain. I'd stay home and serve my community with pride. There was rustling behind me. My legs shook in place instead of fleeing. Fingers clenched around my throat. Teeth sank into flesh.

•   •   •

Your heart stopped beating, but rage burns in your chest. Your eyes popped from your head, but you still follow. The waters of the North Atlantic cool your bodies as you slowly sink in. The Taíno leader, Cacique Agüeybaná, felled by the colonizer in his first life, leads you by the thousands. By the time the enemy sees you rising from the water, it will be too late. The taste of revenge sits on your tongue like sulfides burning off hydrothermal vents. Blood for blood. Death for death. You march on the ocean floor, heading northwest, hungry for the pound of flesh owed to your people.

FLAVOR OF LAB

I TOOK A DEEP BREATH through my nose to calm my nerves and hoped the camera operator was catching my good side. The molecular biology station in my lab was exactly as I'd left it last night—optimized for smooth science: pipettes to my right, already set to the volumes I'd need, and several 50 μL DNA samples ready to be analyzed by gel electrophoresis.

Drayton Love, *Flavor of Lab*'s host, spoke through my earpiece. "Can Cassie Jiménez teach the Zorganks biology? Will it be delicious? Find out—next, on the Lab." Then came the applause of the live studio audience, giddy with expectation. If everything went well, my episode experimenting on alien DNA would boost his ratings and garner funding buzz for my boss's lab. More money would land me the reagents, cell lines, and instruments I needed to finally earn my PhD.

Love cued intro music, an ad for alien scented candles, and then the stage manager waved his hand from behind the camera operator—that was my cue.

"Zorgank technology surpasses ours in the realm of physical sciences," I said, my voice shakier than I wanted it to be. "They mastered space travel before they worked out how genes code for physical traits. Fortunately, their planet is similar to ours, and we know how DNA works." I pointed at the rack of Eppendorf tubes containing the samples. "I conducted PCR on DNA from Zorgank members 27, 49, 59.09876, and $e^{i\pi}$. Today we're going to find out which one of them have the telpo gene."

The stage manager held up a hand, signaling for me to stop talking, and Drayton spoke in my earpiece. "Some Zorganks can use teleportation gates, but only those that have the telpo gene. if a Zorgank without the telpo gene goes into a teleportation gate, they'll show up dead on the other side."

There was an *ahhhh* sound from the audience.

"I'll set an agarose gel to run at 120 volts and make sure the loading dye doesn't run off. The DNA separates by size and will show up like rectangular bands. In our experiment we only expect one band for the telpo gene. Remember that we can only visualize the DNA under UV light, so we'll need to go to another room and ..." I realized I was rambling. *Think about what the viewers care about*, I scolded myself.

I swallowed and tried to focus. "This is the first time this experiment has ever been done. If it's true that the telpo gene is all you need to teleport, then we'll save many Zorgank lives. Right now, they're doing things *the hard way*."

I winked at the camera. Did I just make a dead Zorgank joke? The audience didn't laugh.

"But instead of waiting for this gel to run, we're going to visualize this one instead." I pointed to another light-blue gel floating in a plastic container full of water. I felt like I was on a cooking show. Teach them how to stuff a turkey, then pull a beautifully cooked bird from under the table.

I carried the gel into the small room with a UV light block and turned off the lights.

A piercing alarm went off. For a second, I thought the building was on fire, but it was only in my earpiece. A Zorgank was here.

They were bipedal like us, but resembled ballerinas in controlled pointes when walking. Their skin was turquoise, smooth like ceramic, and stretchy. My guess was that it was made of some sort of natural rubber polymer. They had three eyes—two in the same spot as ours, and a third eye on their forehead. The sharp teeth probably meant they were carnivores.

"Hi." My voice quivered. This was the first time I'd seen one in person. After seeing them on TV so many times I didn't think I'd be intimidated, but they looked bigger in real life.

"I am Zorgank λω and will taste the work." The alien bowed, but it could've just been to enter through the door and not out of politeness.

I narrated what I was doing for the benefit of the viewers, "There will be one bright band per sample near the center of the gel for positive results, so I'll cut a piece from the corner which we don't need."

I scooped the small slice of agarose gel and gave it to the alien. After swallowing, λω smacked his lips and declared, "Solid, delicious science."

Applause broke in my earpiece.

"Now we can visualize the gel. Half of Zorganks have the telpo gene, so it wouldn't surprise me if all four samples were positive. Let's try to visualize at a wavelength of 365 nm."

"Lanes one, three, and four have a positive result ..."

I trailed off, trying to put together what I was seeing. The control reaction I'd chosen was meant to de edgy, but now I was just confused.

"Lane five. The negative control—well, lane five should be empty, because it's my DNA."

Audience: *ooooooooohhhhhhh*

•　　　•　　　•

"The grant we're getting will fund the lab for the rest of your PhD and long after. We're lucky to have gotten this opportunity," my boss wheedled. "And this is a huge opportunity for *you*. Only a few dozen people in all of human history have gotten to travel to an alien world… you'll be a member of a *most* elite club. Plus, you'll be the first human to use a teleportation gate. I can only imagine what kind of treat that will be."

Indeed, I had won the lottery. The genetic lottery. After my experiment, a couple million people, mostly volunteers, had been tested. Only I had the telpo gene.

"Also," my boss interrupted my thoughts. "You're in year seven of grad school, but still don't have enough data to graduate. If this doesn't pan out, you might have to master out."

Blood rushed to my head. If I only got a master's after being here almost a decade, I'd end up on the news and not for a good reason.

"Okay. I'll go. As long as I'm safe," I said.

"They are of course going to make sure you're safe." He fluttered his lips like a man exhausted from stating the obvious.

•　　•　　•

It took a couple of weeks for the Zorganks to build a portal on Earth. They chose one of the green areas at the university. This delighted the administrators and PR staff to no end, but worried all the science and military studies faculty.

Two Zorganks flanked me. They looked friendly enough. They tried to smile and their third eye blinked rapidly.

"I'm ready," I said. Despite probably not needing it, I had insisted on wearing a space suit. The Zorganks were comfortable in our atmosphere, so the opposite was probably true, but I wasn't going to risk it.

The gate was rectangular in shape and around the height of a one-story house. The middle was a hazy purple, like ionized argon.

I clenched my jaw and walked through the gate.

• • •

Instead of an alien vista with talking trees and singing mountains, I was in a huge room. The ceiling, floor, and walls were the cleanest white I'd ever seen. Countertops lined the walls. Each had what looked like a stock pot on top.

Drayton Love appeared in the bottom right of my helmet. "This is the season finale of *Flavor of Lab*. Our Zorgank friends have guaranteed none of the dishes are toxic to humans but which ones are delicious?"

"What?" I thought this was just a visit.

Dozens of Zorganks rappelled from the ceiling like secret agents. Clear plastic cubes hung from their waists. Inside the cubes were a variety of plants and animals.

One Zorgank took out what looked like a tiny fluorescent pig. The Zorgank squeezed the pig and hairy worms squirmed from its back like extruded pasta. I could almost feel the bile in my mouth already. I wished that I was anywhere else, even in a dating show where I'd have to compete to win the affections of some washed-up musician.

"Take a look at your fanbase, Cassie!" Drayton Love's voice was almost a shrill.

Many members of the studio audience were holding signs with things like:

Tasty or don't come back!

Alien food is never vegan!

Among them I saw my boss. He held a sign that said:

Pretty Healthy and Delicious = PhD

I'd better graduate after this.

The Zorganks were signaling me over to try their foods. I took off my helmet, hoping my face would melt from acid in the atmosphere, but knew it wouldn't happen.

The smells weren't half bad at least. There was a scent of fried plantain and garlic that reminded me of mofongo.

"Which experiment will Cassie try first?" Drayton asked.

I was happy I could barely hear his voice coming from the helmet. My suit was covered in cameras I'd been told were for safety, but I was sure they were also transmitting to the studio.

"I want to try a vegetable," I said.

A few of the Zorganks jumped up and down, apparently celebrating my choice.

I walked up to one of them that had a normal-looking root vegetable, maybe a potato and the pot in front of them full of boiling water.

I nodded. The Zorgank dropped the potato in the water.

Two eyes on stalks rose from the water. One of them winked. I swallowed a scream. I heard a commotion from my helmet and imagined my boss egging me on from hundreds of light years away.

"I'll... start with the broth," I said.

The alien gave me a spoon and I sipped. The taste was a mixture of fumes from vinegar and ethyl acetate with the metallic hint of dimethyl sulfoxide. I could see the taste now. I could hear the color white in the walls.

The liquid was a type of fast-acting LSD.

I was in a pool made of butts. Just the cheeks, no holes.

The taste was the experience of all the asses I had kissed throughout my grad school years. I nearly retched. After a few seconds, it was gone. I was normal again.

"You control it," the Zorgank said. "Think of what you want."

I swallowed a second spoonful, looked into the Zorgank's third eye, saw it spin, and concentrated on how good it would taste to write PhD after my name.

It was bliss.

CONSERVATION OF COLD

I OPENED MY EYES and saw my body lying face up on a yellow gurney. My left sleeve was rolled up to the bicep. Smeared blood covered my inside elbow. I tried to stand and yell at the paramedic that I was still here, just a few feet away, prone on the kitchen floor, but the pain in my side rushed to my head and pounded against my temples. I forced air up my throat, bubbling through viscous phlegm. Before I could form words, my throat closed, and my vision became hazy. My body lay unmoving on the gurney, but I—whatever I had become—spasmed against the tiled floor.

Abuela limped down the stairs, out of breath. Her hunched body tilted to the side as she landed on each step. She stood over my body as tears streamed down her face, then slapped the fresh puncture wounds on my arm, yelling, "*¿Por qué hiciste esto?*"

The floor was freezing, and I didn't have enough energy to get up to run away. Even if I did, I would still hear her screaming, blaming me for accidentally killing myself. I managed to bring my hands to my face, but soon realized she couldn't see me. The paramedic signaled Abuela to move away from the gurney, and despite her anger and desperation, she did. He placed his shaking palms between my breasts, and using his entire weight, compressed my chest, then placed two fingers on my neck. His face tensed. Abuela followed the paramedic as he rushed me out of the front door. Ambulance sirens wailed, disappearing down the street as I lay on the cold tiles.

•　　•　　•

It took a long time for the shock to wear off, and even longer for me to lose all hope of being revived or returning to my body. I was able to sit. Pain, disbelief, and stress all present. Yet something I had when alive was missing, a force so strong that I considered it an emotion. The desire to get high when things got difficult, to steady a downer with an upper had disappeared. I died, but I was free of my addiction. Abuela would feel better when I told her. Like some Puerto Ricans of her age group, her religion combined Catholicism, Santería, and several forms of magic, sprinkled with her own unique beliefs. I could only imagine how concerned she was over my so-called soul.

My hands didn't pass through the walls like in the movies, nor did I sink through the floor into oblivion. I was invisible but solid. I'd be able to write a message on the wall with the paint we kept in the porch. She'd freak out, but reading a message was probably less disturbing than hearing me speak. My footsteps were silent as I walked towards the screen door leading outside, where my real body had crossed through the porch and then to the ambulance.

I didn't see any cars parked on the street, but soon enough, the neighbors would get home from their jobs, find out I had overdosed on heroin, then run over, crying to Abuela. *I'm so sorry for your loss. Alicia was such a bright girl.* Then they'd pat Abuela's wrinkled hands and say, *I'm sure God has a reason for taking her so young.* Of course, when they'd gone back home, out of earshot from the outside world, their tongues would fall off with the weight of hot gossip. *I knew something bad was going to happen to that girl. Doing drugs all the time. To make matters worse, she was an atheist. I don't want to say this, but I'm afraid that if she didn't embrace Jesus before departing, she's in a bad place now.*

Cold air blew into the house. I hugged myself and shivered. It reminded me of vacationing in Boston during winter. The temperature in Puerto Rico never dropped this low, so the cold had to be a consequence of my condition. It was sunny outside, and after writing my message, I could take a walk to warm myself up.

I pulled the screen door's handle. It didn't move. I grabbed my wrist with my other hand, pulling until I trembled in place. The flimsy screen door designed to stop flies and vermin didn't budge. I tried other doors that led to the bathroom, kitchen pantry, and backyard. None of them moved. Smaller items, like the pen I found under the sofa, were also infinitely heavy. I kicked and punched every object around me, begging for something to at least stir and acknowledge my existence. I didn't get fatigued but eventually became bored of taking my anger out on the house. I wandered aimlessly until I found myself in front of the living room mirror.

Nothing. I had no reflection. I waved my hands, but sunlight coming from the windows passed through me, uninterrupted. My pale and naked body was only visible to me.

•　　　•　　　•

Abuela came back hours later, giving me enough time to figure out the nature of what I was. In a nutshell, I had no mass. Without mass, I couldn't exert force, explaining my inability to move things. Light didn't interact with me either, further supporting my assumption. Yet I had awareness and could interact with objects, even if it was just to be hindered by them. Dr. Miguel Suárez, the man who was shepherding me towards earning my Ph.D. in biochemistry, would be proud. Even in death, I still approached problems with a scientific mind. Unfortunately, he'd never find out.

"Alicia..." Abuela said. Her voice cracked as she said my name. *"Te suicidaste con una sobredosis. Estás en el infierno."*

I turned and saw her standing on the threshold to the kitchen. I tried to speak and explain to her that I hadn't killed myself and that overdosing could hardly be considered suicide. Instead, I became dizzy as the words formed in my throat. I felt like pulling my hair from the frustration of not being able to communicate. I needed to tell her. My being here was what mattered. Her religion was giving her more grief than closure. Chances were, Hell didn't even exist.

Tears ran down her wrinkled face. Her eyes focused on the living room wall as if expecting a miracle to occur. A string of wooden beads, her rosary, was coiled around her forearm. The room grew colder still. I tried to force words out but lost my balance and landed on my knees. No sound left my mouth. It took several seconds for me to recover. She raised her shaky arms to pray and lowered her head.

I got closer. A barely noticeable substance surrounded her like an aura. Translucent, yellow gas rippled from her arms. I hovered both hands over her forearm. The gas was hot. She warmed me like a campfire. I ran my hands through the colored heat, parting the waves, absorbing some warmth. The back of my hands prickled. Her heat diffused into my body, relaxing me. My mouth salivated. The energy was delicious. Without thinking, I grasped Abuela's wrist, squeezing as hard as I could. She screamed. Abuela's gaze locked with mine.

"Alicia!" She flung her arm loose.

I stumbled back, catching a glimpse of myself in the living room mirror before disappearing again. She looked at her wrist with wide eyes and crossed herself with her other hand, the wooden Jesus dangling from the string of beads. My body itched for more heat.

"*Un demonio enmascarado,*" she said. "*Padre nuestro, que estás en los cielo, santificado sea tu nombre...*" She darted upstairs, repeating the Lord's Prayer in a loop. Abuela had lived in the states for more than a decade before moving back home and was fully bilingual, but she always prayed in Spanish.

I rushed after her, pushing the curtain at the base of the staircase; instead of acting as a concrete wall, the stringed beads moved aside. Abuela looked back at what had to look like the beads moving from their own volition. She whimpered, cradling her wrist against her chest, and ran. The cold gripped my legs again, and I stumbled on the steps. She prayed louder, rushing into her room, then slammed the door shut.

When we connected, I wanted to hug her, tell her I loved her, to say, "Everything will be all right, abuelita," but the feeling of euphoria had overwhelmed me, and speaking, at least trying to, knocked me off balance. Despite my effort, my situation had gotten worse. After seeing me, Abuela now believed I was a demon in disguise since in her head the real me—my soul—had to be somewhere in Hell being poked by some little red man with a pitchfork. None of this made sense to me, but in the end, everyone's religion was whatever they wanted it to be.

I heard her door open but still didn't climb the stairs. How could I? If I couldn't talk, there was no excuse to get close and touch her except for how good it made me feel. And touching her also hurt her. Despite her pain, I didn't trust myself to not grab her again if I came too close.

On the second floor, echoes of Abuela's weeping filled the hallway. She stomped around. The house went silent after she finished whatever she was doing, shutting her door again, and I mustered enough courage to go upstairs.

The other rooms and bathrooms were open. Abuela insisted on airing the house, keeping the doors open when a room was unoccupied. She claimed the smell of stuffiness and used socks accumulated otherwise.

I found my room as I had left it. Every piece of clothes, make-up, and my school backpack in their usual place, as if expecting me to come back from the dead and continue my routine. The bottom drawer in my dresser, where I kept my stash—and hid my special spoon just before the heroin kicked in and killed me—was closed, unexplored. Yet Abuela knew I had drugs. Maybe not in that specific drawer but somewhere.

During the last few years, she'd thrown around enough innuendos about how bad habits can shape a person into something they're not, a collection of warnings to persuade me to quit, to stop coming home with bloodshot eyes and slurred speech. I ignored her, thinking my vices were under control.

Drugs, especially stronger stuff, were only for special occasions, like when the stress of lab work threatened to drive me crazy after years of sixteen-hour workdays, running experiments six days a week, while being unappreciated by everyone outside of science.

I'd started with alcohol like everyone else, then marihuana when too much booze ruined my digestion. I skipped through cocaine and—only on special occasions—landed on a needle. The whole thing felt like a repeating series of accidents, as if I was tripping on the same rock on my walk to school every day. But I wasn't going to use drugs forever. The plan was to quit right after graduation.

I sat on my bed for hours, fidgeting while thinking of my situation. It never made a sound, the creaking of worn, rusty springs absent. Instead, a chill spiraled up my spine like fingers flicking air out of a syringe. The clock on my room wall read seven.

Eventually, I stood to look outside my window. Black bows hung from the front door of every house, a sign of respect to the recently deceased. Two black ribbons stretched from each bow and piled into small mounds. They must've bought them in the same store, or probably one of the neighbors bought one for everyone. I wouldn't be surprised if it had been Abuela who gifted the bows, asking nicely that they be hung. All traces of Abuela's heat left me, and the pleasure went with it. Only the anger after seeing the neighborhood's hypocrisy lingered.

The past few years, I'd managed the drive home while intoxicated more than once, only to park too far from the sidewalk, open the door, and vomit on the street as tears ran down my face. On a few occasions, the neighbors called the cops. The neighbors hated me, called me a negative influence on their kids, despite the fact I never talked to any of them. None of them were perfect either. I always urged Abuela to call the police when the loud spousal fights or drunken parties stretched late into the night, but she'd just shrug. *God rewards those who turn the other cheek*, she'd always say, as if her patience was a down payment for going to Heaven.

Something caught my foot as I turned from the window. A red seven-day candle with a drawing of a saint on it stood beside my bed. In a wooden frame beside the candle, I saw a picture of me as a little girl, missing my two front teeth and wearing a proud smile. Abuela must have set this up after I touched her. I crouched down until my knees reached my head. Red, blood-thick wax pooled below the burning wick. The flame flickered in an uninterrupted, random pattern. I waved the back of my hand near the fire.

"Te amo, Alicia." Abuela stood in the doorway. This was the second time she addressed me after my death as if a part of her knew I was close. I brought my fingertips closer to the flame, then rested my cheek on my left knee, waiting for her to turn and leave. If she thought I was a demon, I couldn't imagine how she'd react after seeing me, spine taut against my skin, slouched in front of my proffering. She turned, and I closed my eyes, then cupped the flame in my palm, but nothing happened. The flame felt cold as metal. I hadn't considered the possibility that only human heat affected me.

The need for a satisfying heat high only increased after the failed attempt with the candle. Abuela shut my door before I reached her. I considered calling out to her, but the thought of speaking made me nauseous. I stood in front of the door. Unlike when I had a body, and worked long hours standing in front of a lab bench, my legs didn't fall asleep, the stiffness in my neck never came. Still as a statue, I waited. A gnawing need to absorb heat kept me company.

•   •   •

The next morning, Abuela slowly turned the doorknob as a voice came from outside, stopping her before she fully opened my door.

"*¡Voy!*" Abuela yelled. She left the door ajar. Even turning my body sideways, I wouldn't fit through. Outside my window, I saw Cynthia, one of the neighbors from across the street, walking from our mailbox with a package cradled in her side. *Bringing Abuela her mail?* She had to be up to something. I squinted, looking at Cynthia's house. Aluminum screens behind the window panes blocked my view. But I knew they were there: Cynthia's sisters, Amanda, and Carla—what I called the gossip patrol—keeping watch. I heard Abuela swing the porch gate open. Cynthia walked into the house.

If I found a way to get close to Cynthia, I could feed on her heat. Abuela felt something when I touched her, surprise and pain filling her cataract filmed eyes after I grabbed her wrist. I was dead but not unfeeling. The fact that it felt good to grab her only added to my guilt. However, Cynthia's health wasn't my concern. And I wouldn't surprise myself after becoming visible. With enough heat, I'd probably be visible for a while. I could smile and wave to Abuela, convincing her I wasn't an evil demon. Maybe we could even leave the house together and find others like me. Statistically, I couldn't be the only one; no one was that unique.

I had to admit I was also curious. Cynthia was around my age. Perhaps if I touched her, my high would be different. The experience might be more intense, the difference between a few sips of beer or pounding several tequila shots in rapid succession, or maybe, a young person's heat changed the high altogether, and I'd trampoline from the drowsiness caused by Xanax to the jaw twisting strength of cocaine.

I grabbed the doorknob, then pulled with both hands. Nothing happened. A way for me to move objects had to exist because I'd been able to move the curtain earlier. I concentrated, willing strength to accumulate in my fingers. A paralyzing cold spread from my toes, feet, and up my legs as if I was slowly dipping myself into an icy lake. White vapor rose from the doorknob as I squeezed it. I pulled. The door started to open, moving towards me at a snail pace. I leaned back. The door swung towards me, and I fell backward.

After sitting up, I realized my knees were locked in position. I tried to stand, but my legs didn't move. I cupped my right knee with both hands to force the joint to bend, but my palms sizzled with a freezing burn.

What I was became clear. Words like ghosts, spirit, angel, and demon were useless, blanket statements so generalizable and loaded with preconceptions that the terms themselves lost meaning. A rigorous definition was more useful. I had died and become a Carnot engine of sorts, an instrument that transformed heat into mechanical energy. The heat I extracted from living people also made me visible. I smiled, thinking of my research on fluorescent molecules. The shiny dots became brighter as the temperature of their environment increased. Not even the dead escaped the laws of thermodynamics. Still grinning, I flipped onto my stomach, dragging myself out of the room like a slithering snake.

"Hola, Doña Amelia," Cynthia said, her voice echoing up the stairs.

"*Gracias por venir,*" Abuela said.

"Claro." Cynthia giggled.

What was so good about Cynthia coming over? I'd told Abuela a thousand times not to trust the neighbors, but every time I gave her a reason, she'd just say that talking about people who gossip counted as gossip. She claimed a better approach was to be the best person you can be and give nothing interesting to talk about. Then she'd give me that look that said she knew I gave too much to talk about.

I slapped the floor with my clammy hands, pulling myself towards the stairs. My paralyzed legs dragged like the tall gas cylinders in my lab. If Cynthia came upstairs, I'd grab her ankles and absorb all the heat I could. I needed to warm up my legs, in addition to a nice buzz.

"*El mapo está en el pantry,*" Abuela said. *The mop is in the pantry*. Cynthia made a ruckus taking the mop out. I paused. Maybe I was being too harsh and overconfident in my judgment. It was hard to imagine Cynthia volunteered for housework just to find things to create a scandal over. I lugged back to my room.

When I was alive, cleaning was my responsibility. Looking for patches of dust that I'd missed, like a crime scene investigator, was Abuela's favorite hobby. She hadn't given me cooking, yard work, or any other chores. I didn't even pay rent. She told me to focus on school, saying she was proud I'd be the first doctor in the family. Unlike the rest of my family and friends, she never cracked a joke about a Ph.D. in biochemistry not being a real doctor. At times, her belief in me was the only force keeping me in pursuit of my career. And now, I'd never graduate, never make the only person who really cared proud. I was only missing one experiment to have enough data for a publication, immortalizing my name among the scientific community. My work was wasted, or worse, another person in the lab would finish it, and push me down the author list, maybe even take my name off completely since I didn't need publications to advance my career anymore.

Back in my room, my kindergarten-self smiled back at me from the framed picture. Most worries I had when alive had disappeared. Things that kept me up at night like the search for jobs after graduation, how I'd struggle to kick my drug habits when the time came, were unimportant. The question of how long it would take to save enough money to rent my own place seemed absurd now. Yet, I still couldn't imagine being as happy as I looked in the picture. So much had been left undone. The happiness I saw in the picture stemmed from a child's ignorance and not a sense of professional or personal accomplishments.

Cynthia grunted. She stood outside my room, barefoot on the tiled floor, using both hands to carry a large bucket with a mop inside. Water splashed on the floor when she set it down. Abuela hadn't entered my room after leaving the candle and my picture. She hadn't cleaned any part of the house either. In fact, I couldn't remember the last time I saw her eat. Her body had abruptly become frailer since I died. The hunch on her back curving a few degrees in less than two days. I didn't need to like Cynthia to recognize the favor she was doing Abuela.

I crawled under my bed to avoid bumping into the mop, starting to accept my condition as permanent and unfixable. Cynthia sat on my bed with a creaking sound. Her ankles released a faint blue vapor. I leaned my head in, the energy caressing my cheeks. The hairs behind my neck stood as I inhaled silky ribbons of blue, gaseous heat. A prickling sensation ran down my legs. Cynthia giggled and shuffled her feet. For a second, I thought she felt me close, but instead of looking under the bed, she stood and walked towards the window.

She laughed louder, then mumbled something about a ridiculous old lady.

I pulled my upper body from under the bed and saw her standing, hips tilted, pointing her phone at the candle and my portrait, snapping pictures. She knocked on the metal window panes, calling out to her sisters, who no doubt came running to their own windows like drooling dogs. I started to tremble, biting on the inside of my lips. She lifted the phone to the window—as if her idiot sisters had long-range vision—telling them how much they were going to laugh when they saw the pictures she was taking. Did she not care that Abuela might be within earshot?

She turned to leave, still sliding her finger on the phone, probably looking at the picture through different filters, or adding sparkles around the candle, increasing the juiciness of her find. I slammed my fists against the floor. How could she be so disrespectful? Cynthia skipped from the window, still laughing. It was clear she had no intention to clean. I lunged, grabbing both of her ankles. She squealed, then dropped her phone. Pleasure rippled through me. Every cell in my body excited simultaneously, the first time high of every drug I'd used when alive, mixed with the gut-clenching spasms of an orgasm. Cynthia screamed. I turned my head, stared straight into her eyes, and bit her calf, sinking my teeth deep into muscle. Her heat flowed down my throat, a sweet and warm liquid that filled me with bliss.

She screamed senseless dribble. Thick strands of saliva flew from her mouth. Her arms swung wildly over her head as if wanting to defend her but not knowing how. Ceramic boxes on top of my dresser shattered against the floor, spilling jewelry everywhere. I held for a long time, but the high only got better, not limited by the bioelectrical saturation limit of a nervous system.

I whispered her name: "Cynthia."

Dark blotches formed at the edge of my vision. My strength seeped away, and Cynthia freed one of her legs, then the other. I heard her name from far away. Her sisters must have heard the racket and were calling to her. I reached out, trying to grab the cell phone, and text Abuela while the tingling heat ran through my body, but everything went black.

•   •   •

It was nighttime when I woke up. Cynthia must have rushed back to her house. Hopefully, she would spend the next few years crying herself to sleep in terror, visiting psychologists until she convinced herself that what she'd seen wasn't real; perhaps some residual drugs were lying around in my room, and she'd hallucinated after inhaling them; maybe the stress from a neighbor dying had made her brain fabricate illusions. Whatever lie eventually comforted her, the bite marks guaranteed it would take a while for normalcy to set in.

My legs worked again, so I walked around the second floor of the house. Abuela was in her room, reading her Bible while she lay on the bed. I couldn't tell if her hands were shaking from old age or because of the aftermath of what I had done. The ten o'clock news blared on the TV that sat on a table across from her. On days that I came home drunk or high, which lately had become every day, she cranked the TV volume even higher, giving me a small hint that I had done something wrong and didn't deserve to sleep in peace.

Seeing her made my eyes water. How was I supposed to deal with the loneliness of death? The despair in my heart climbed my throat and quivered in my lips. She was so close but unreachable, untouchable. I had taken so much for granted when I was alive, thinking that she would always be there, that I'd have the rest of my life to discover and share new scientific phenomena, that dying of a drug overdose was something that happened to people who weren't careful, and not to scientists in training who measured micrograms daily. I'd also managed to be irresponsible with my high during death. Knowing that talking somehow ruined my vision and balance hadn't stopped me from whispering to scare Cynthia. The lesson of self-control was lost on me.

Now I was dead, and the high was gone. Only the guilt of the recently sobered who realized they had fallen off the wagon remained. I was trapped in a house where the only way to get around was to suck heat off a living person. Instead of a sophisticated machine, an efficient engine, I had become a parasite, feeding off living things for pleasure. I existed in a vacuum with no purpose. No ecosystem.

Abuela had been right. Everyone had stress, and sometimes the difference between swimming in an endless ocean of anxiety or drowning in a glass of water was the perspective we took. What I missed about life now was exactly that stress, the uncertainty, the challenge to be a successful scientist, a better person.

I stood in Abuela's doorway and resented her. She could've been more aggressive. If I didn't want to see, she should have pried my eyes open, even organized an intervention. She could've been more direct.

I shook my head. It was time I took responsibility for my actions. Blaming my problems on anything except myself, dealing with them immaturely, such as numbing my mind with drugs, had already killed me.

Abuela had been right in other ways as well: we only had the power to change ourselves. What had I gained by hurting Cynthia? Abuela would only be ostracized by the community. Whispers of her being a witch, the house being haunted, running up and down the gossip wire. Tears ran down my face, taking the last of my heat with them. The cold filled me completely.

I sat at the foot of the bed, careful to be far enough from Abuela so she wouldn't stretch and accidentally touch me. We watched the weather until a coughing fit made her sit up. She covered her mouth with her white gown. Fresh blood stood out stark against the whiteness of the cloth. The urge to touch her clawed up my stomach, then concentrated in my temples. I resisted. Addiction had beat me in life and followed me into death, but I wouldn't succumb a second time—

Abuela coughed again. And it occurred to me: she might join me soon. This time I'd follow every piece of advice to the letter. She had always been curious about what I did at school. There would be enough time for me to teach her science. And together, grandmother and granddaughter, we'd explore this new phase of existence.

•   •   •

As if by design, Abuela died that night. I first noticed that her chest had stopped rising and falling, then I grazed my fingers over her cheeks. Touching her was the same as any other object in the house. Lifeless. Her heat was gone.

The beaded curtain at the bottom of the stairs jingled. She must have learned how to use her heat already. Impressive. Or maybe people that died at different ages became a different kind of ghost. I couldn't wait to learn about it.

I stood from the bed, thinking as fast as I could. How could I communicate with Abuela? I needed to be as loving as possible and not demon-like.

Abuela stood naked at the top of the stairs. Loose skin hung from her body. She looked the same as when alive, but I knew she felt no pain. I smiled, then waved at her like a parent waves at a child. Her jaw hung open, her eyes full of recognition.

She gagged, making a wet sound deep in her throat. I moved a bit closer, with my index finger on my lips.

"*¿Donde? Demonio,*" she said slowly, like someone struggling to speak through a heart attack. She fell on her knees. I kneeled in front of her.

She whispered, "*Paraíso …*" The wrinkles on her face squeezed together. "*… mi paraíso.*" Her eyes locked with mine. She pointed towards the ceiling.

I understood. She had died and not gone to Heaven. Instead, she thought she'd joined a shapeshifting demon. Still kneeling, she clenched her fists and punched her thighs as if punishing her unresponsive legs. I tried to catch her attention by waving my hands. I looked into her eyes. Instead of my Abuela staring back, I only saw rage. I tried to stand, but she lunged at me, pushing me by the neck until I fell on my back.

She yelled, "*¡Tu culpa!*" *Your fault!*

Abuela sat on my stomach and slammed my head against the floor, repeatedly, until I heard my skull crack. I felt no pain, but she was draining my energy.

I tried to suck some heat back, but I was too weak. She had too much of an advantage. Her tongue ran over her lips, like someone remembering how delicious food was. I tried to wiggle from under her, anything to resist the efflux of heat from my body. Abuela moved her hands from my neck to my face, threatening to squeeze out the last of my heat. I looked at her, begging her to stop, but the patience she had in life was extinguished. She buried her thumbs into my eyes. Vitreous liquid mixed with tears ran down the side of my head. She slammed my head against the floor again. When the last drops of my heat diffused into her, I plummeted through the floor like a traitor cast from paradise.

•   •   •

I have yet to find an escape from this place. I walked in the cold until I found the wall. As far as I can tell, it stretches to infinity on either side. A sense of satisfaction is the first thing I'd feel if you told me you were able to read this writing. I had to rest my wrist on my forehead to try and keep the sentences level. I still can't see and don't know if my blood sticks to the wall or just runs off. I'm not even sure if the wall is white or another color light enough to serve as a good medium for writing on. At least, my blood seems to never run out.

It took me a long time to think of biting my thumb open and using the blood to write—no, to publish—my story. Unfortunately, this never occurred to me while in Abuela's house.

Please, if you find this, call out to me. I'll call back. I can speak now, scream even, but no one hears. I don't want to be in this Hell by myself. I can't tell if the rheumy running down my face is from weeping or something else. I am so cold, but I won't touch you. I've learned my lesson. I promise.

I need to find a way out of this place and tell Abuela that I love her! I don't blame her for what happened. In a way, I was part demon in life already. She'd spent her life knowing that suffering and pain were rewarded with an unimaginably happy afterlife, but after dying, she hadn't entered through golden gates into a garden of infinite bliss; she only saw me. She had no reason to behave like a good Christian anymore.

If you are reading this, Abuela, I'm sorry. This is not Heaven. But I've confirmed there is a place that can be called Hell, opening the possibility that an opposite realm exists. If we meet here, let's pray together. I hope I can make you proud.

Alicia M. López
Ph.D. Candidate in Biochemistry
Draft #177 of "A 25-Year-Old Woman Experiences Life After Death: A Case Study."

THE GREATER SECRETS OF CARBOCATIONS

M Y LAB BENCH WAS the cleanest it had ever been. The pipettes were on their rack, in order of increasing volume capacity, the glass amber bottles containing dozens of compounds in alphabetical order. Years of accumulated dirty glassware had been cleaned and shelved elsewhere.

After my thesis advisor, Dr. Ramos, died last week, a few local reporters had come in to interview my lab, me and Mara, for the town's newspaper. Every year, my advisor had volunteered some of his students—including me three times—for science demonstrations at the local high school, which I hated since doing so didn't directly help me towards graduating. This had made him a local celebrity in the school system, and he was well liked in the town.

The Biochemistry department's chair had come in hours before the reporters, and with tears in his eyes, yelled at me and Mara to clean up his best friend's lab.

Today was the first day I'd come back to work after the funeral, and before I finished my organic synthesis reactions, the bench would be a mess all over again.

The door to the lab banged against the wall and startled me as someone walked in. I dropped an Erlenmeyer flask in the fume hood and spilled hexane all over. Not a terribly toxic accident, but it added another hour of work. The small amounts of evaporated hexane that escaped the fume hood smelled like boiling grease.

"Trying to get a workout in before lab?" I asked Mara while carefully picking up broken glass. I didn't have to turn from the hood to look at her. We'd worked together for four years, and I could tell it was her from the footfall.

"You need to see something." Her voice broke.

When I turned, she was already sitting at her desk. I couldn't see her, but she sounded as stressed as I felt.

"Give me a sec," I said.

"Did Dr. Ramos ever seem weird to you? Like a man who's into the occult or mysticism. Any kind of magic?"

"What? Like a wizard?"

"Sure, like a wizard," she said in that way I knew her eyes were rolling upwards, which was unfair because she'd brought up the magic stuff in the first place.

The boss had been a staunch atheist, as far as I knew. But who knows, maybe he'd lost it near the end or had spent his life keeping secrets. With enough practice, people got really good at keeping secrets. I'd kept my feelings hidden from Mara for nearly half a decade and was willing to do so for the rest of my life to not risk losing our friendship.

"You need to watch this. Before you ask, it isn't a Deepfake or any kind of simulation. I made sure," she said.

Now, I was curious. Had a grad student—or even better, a faculty member—been recorded doing something embarrassing? I finished pushing the broken glass to a corner in the hood and walked over to her desk.

She was disheveled; her eyes puffy from crying, face breaking out, hair tied back in a ponytail with loose strands escaping here and there. She looked like she spent her nights crying herself to sleep.

I sat on a chair beside her, wanting to hug her and say I was here for her no matter what. I couldn't. Lab romances were notorious for ending up in meltdowns, even when they didn't suffer under the scrutiny of other students and faculty. And that's only if she reciprocated, which wasn't guaranteed either.

"What's wrong?" I asked.

"This can't be real, but it is." She opened her laptop, and plugged in a jump drive. There was a single video file on the drive.

In the video, Dr. Ramos sat in a metal chair in an otherwise empty room. The wall and floor behind him were white. He held a deck of cards in his left hand. For a few seconds, he didn't move. Then he spoke:

"Traveling is difficult, but even more difficult are those journeys that require a transformation." He stopped talking.

This was a sick joke.

I had already seen him transform. He'd changed from a healthy man to a sick one, and then to a body in a suit for his funeral in the span of three weeks. I looked away, trying to focus on my bench and on my science.

"There is nothing you need to learn for a theurgic ascent, only remember what you have forgotten. I can help you guys."

After he said *you guys*, my stomach sank, and the hairs on my arms stood up. He said it in the same tone as when addressing us. Worse, it was the same tone he used when trying to be helpful, when laser focused on mentoring his students.

"Where did you find that jump drive?" I asked Mara.

"It's not over. Watch."

Ramos didn't move for a few seconds, then he pulled a card from the deck and showed it to the camera. Mara inhaled like she had just recently developed asthma.

The card showed an old, bearded man, who looked a bit like Santa Claus, sitting on a throne. He wore red clothes, a golden crown, and had what I could only imagine was a magic wand in his right hand. The Roman numeral IV was written on the top, while THE EMPEROR was written at the bottom of the card.

This was like sitting in front of a wannabe psychic at a cheap carnival.

"Don't be afraid," said Ramos. He opened his mouth a couple of centimeters more than looked natural and shoved the card into his mouth and swallowed. The video went black.

Mara was taking shallow breaths through her nose. Her gaze was unfocused and distant, as if her brain was busy scrubbing out what she'd seen, so she wouldn't go into shock, which would be bad because we were training for doctorates in biochemistry, not medicine.

"I found the jump drive in my desk drawer. This is the fifth time I've seen it. I needed to show it to someone I trust in case it's me who's going crazy," she said.

"It's creepy. Like, really creepy." I had nothing else to say and lingered on the fact that I was someone she trusted.

Tears started to run down her cheeks. Part of me felt she was overreacting. There were hundreds of spooky videos on YouTube. You'd think people would be numb to "unexplainable" recordings, but the relationship between her and Ramos had been different than mine. She really enjoyed spending time in his office, going over experiments, trying to get that one result that would make them famous. It was much more admirable than my laziness. Seeing him after he died was enough to push her over the edge. Honestly, I was a little disturbed too, but needed to keep it together for both of us.

I knew how I could cheer her up.

We both worked on volatile compounds made by plants, and knew which molecules produced specific smells. To pass the time, we'd often challenge each other to guess the smell of whatever we were working with. Monoterpenes such as α- and β-pinene, R- and S-limonene, eucalyptol, myrcene, carvone, terpineol, menthol, camphene, geraniol, and linalool—just to name a few—were the easiest to identify.

I opened a bottle of R-limonene, the major component in orange-peel oil, and wafted the mouth of the bottle to spread the limonene around.

"Do you smell that?" I asked.

She slammed her fists on her laptop's keyboard. The screen went black. "I don't give a fuck."

"Sorry." I recapped the bottle.

"No. It's okay. I'm stressed out." She smiled the smile I liked. "I think I just broke my computer. Can we use yours to watch it again?"

"Yeah," I said, unsure why she wanted to see it again.

"This is gonna be my sixth time seeing it."

I pulled my laptop from my bag and hinted that maybe it wasn't a good idea to rewatch a video like that.

I hesitated before plugging in the jump drive.

"I scanned it for viruses too," she said.

Ramos started talking and Mara paced around. I didn't understand what the problem was until near the end, when he pulled a different card from the deck. Card V, THE HIEROPHANT.

•　　　•　　　•

"Drugs?" I asked. "If it isn't a Deepfake or CGI or whatever. Maybe the lab is laced with hallucinogens."

"They are coming up in order, Gerardo. It's the Major Arcana of the tarot," Mara said.

"You really looked into this," I said.

She was one of those people who could make sense of, and solve, any problem, not only scientific ones.

I stood and went to my bench. My hands were shaking. I couldn't do experiments like this.

She stayed in front of my laptop, still as a statue. "Anyway, how could it be drugs if we both saw the same thing? You think every surface is coated in DMT or psilocybin and our hallucinations just happened to match?"

"Okay. I get it. I'm just trying to think it through. What do you think?"

"I have no idea how this could be done," she said. "Even if I did, it doesn't matter. I deleted the video file last night." She paused. "Then I dreamt that a man wearing a jester's costume touched the jump drive and recovered the video. I could hear the bells on his shoes and hat. It was the Fool... and he had your face, but it was twisted and disgusting. Guess what I saw on the drive the next day?"

I hoped her comment meant that I was good looking.

At the very least, we could check how reproducible that was. "Delete it now," I said.

She did. I came over, pulled out the drive and walked to the lab computer. "There's nothing on it and hasn't been plugged into this machine."

The video file was there.

Mara bit her lip. "This doesn't make sense. I'm scared. It can't be real."

"Wait. This is the lab. He obviously pulled the same trick on every computer and—"

"What trick? Fuck. A super trick before he died? Or do you think he travels from the astral plane to tinker with our electronics every time we're not looking? Maybe he became supreme God of the cosmos, and before he goes on to create new universes, he wants to practice using his powers by trolling us?"

"I get it," I said. "I know nothing makes sense."

She scoffed and raised her hands.

That gesture pissed me off. Whatever. I hit PLAY.

Same thing all over again. This time, he pulled card VI, THE LOVERS. I took a deep breath and thought, *if only*.

Something else had changed. It was small, but there.

"You saw that?" I asked Mara.

"What? That THE LOVERS came up?"

She wasn't even looking. "Yeah. Also, he moved," I said.

"What? The man on the card or Dr. Ramos? Be specific."

I swallowed down my sarcastic, specific retort. "Ramos. Like he coughed or something, after eating the card. A small gesture, but it was there. It's not the same video. It must be a gag."

She laughed and said, "A gag makes sense." She was happy to deliver her own sarcasm.

I lost it and raised my voice. "Who gives a shit? So there's a weird video that doesn't make sense. Spend five minutes on Reddit and you'll find a hundred more." The keyboard was creaking in my grip. I was about to twist it like a pretzel.

She tilted her head down. "I'm sorry."

We'd spent every single weekday and most weekends in the same place, sharing jokes, commiserating about grad school. The fact that she only apologized when I was about to break something made me feel more guilty. Was this a sign of romantic tension between us? Did she even suspect how I felt?

I wanted to say something, but neither of us spoke for a long time.

•　　•　　•

She wanted to see the video on a bigger screen to catch every detail, so we borrowed her mom's laptop—which also served as a control for the possibility Ramos had rigged the lab computers—and connected it to the projector we kept in the lunchroom for group meetings. The lunchroom smelled like stale potato chips.

We sat side by side and hit PLAY. Then, we hit PLAY again and again. We watched our boss pull cards, one by one. Each time, the card was different, his final gesture also changed. By card XV, THE DEVIL, Ramos was coughing like he had emphysema, after eating the card.

"It's late. Let's take a break until tomorrow," I said, past the point of freaking out. My mind was numb. Something unexplainable was happening, but it only looked like magic because of our ignorance. Once we knew how it worked, it would become science. We might wake up tomorrow and all this would click into place; the universe would make sense again.

"No. Tomorrow's Monday. People will be here. The Major Arcana goes up to number twenty-one. We'll hit the end soon." She looked at me and smiled. She was so focused now, obsessed even. Her determination was contagious. In science, you were either obsessed or lucky, and trying to tell the difference was a waste of time; time that was better spent obsessing or being lucky.

This was the woman for me. After tonight, I would tell her. Fuck gossip and taboos. Ramos had taught me two important lessons. First: Always do the best science you can, because quality is better than ephemeral, flashy bullshit. Second: Don't wait until you die to speak your mind. You might have to record yourself babbling about nonsense.

After card XIX, THE SUN, we were so close to each other, we might as well have been sharing a chair; I could feel the heat coming off of her skin.

Ramos was coughing up a brown mist now. The speech was the same. Theurgic ascent; journey; your soul needs to remember.

Card XX, JUDGMENT. Throughout the coughing fit, I could hear singing. It sounded like Mara's voice.

I felt like we were being watched.

The scientific assuredness left me. I was cold and scared. I wanted to run away and cry. Mara was crying, her face red and swollen. Had she heard it?

This time, the video restarted itself.

Card XXI, THE WORLD. After swallowing the card, Ramos started to projectile vomit a brown stream of dirt. His chest heaved, his stomach bulged and contracted, but the stream was constant. I started to cry. The Mara who was singing in the video started to laugh. I tried to keep my mouth from quivering, but instead my whole body started trembling. I had to pee. My chest hurt.

The dirt now covered Ramos and continued to rise.

A door flung open in our lab.

"Close your eyes. Don't look," Mara said. She grabbed my hand. "It's not real. Wait for it to go away."

I closed my eyes.

I needed to tell her now. If other people didn't like it, then fuck 'em, fuck my PhD, my career, fuck the universe…

"Mara—"

She grabbed my hand and squeezed. "Do you smell that?"

I did. It was the smell of rain. The smell of the earth. The smell of water falling on bacteria in the soil and killing them. The smell you think of when you think of rain is the smell of bacteria bursting. It was the smell of petrichor, the scent of death.

"Geosmin, a sesquiterpene," I said.

She squeezed my hand harder.

I recognized the footfall approaching us; it belonged to a man who knew more now than I would ever know. A man I wish would know my hate for him and love for Mara.

"Mara." I was crying again. "Mara, I love you. I'm sorry, but I love you."

My ears and mouth filled with dirt. I opened my eyes, but couldn't see anything.

Mara's hand was slipping. I dug my nails into her skin, and she dug her nails into mine; I felt love mixed with desperation. I would never let go.

"Remember." Cold fingers closed around my other hand.

ONE STEP FORWARD, TWO STEPS STARWAYS, THREE STEPS PLOP!

THE STARSHARD HAD BEEN LOST for eons, and no living creature knew of its location, but I had a plan. After searching through various star systems, I learned that some Earthlings possessed unnatural powers, such as speaking to the dead. Surely there had to be at least one spirit, somewhere, who could help me.

Impatient to visit one of these so-called psychics, I only skimmed a few aspects of human culture: biology, socioeconomics, and John Travolta.

I synthesized human clothing and artificial skin on my ship. The human ballet shoes I wore constricted my toes but looked too stylish to ignore. My human mask felt too tight around the neck region. Unfortunately, there was no time to fix it. The Pink Nebulae's dance competition was in one Earth day. I needed to win. If I didn't find the Starshard in time, my dancing career would be ruined, and I'd be forced to get what my friends called *a real job*.

●　　　●　　　●

A curtain composed of multicolored, stringed beads concealed the entrance to the psychic's shop. I nimbly climbed up a few steps but tripped on the doorstep, crossed the hanging beads, landing in a front split, arms above my head in the shape of a triangle. Improvised choreographies had become second nature when my equilibrium faltered. The movements were sloppy but still more graceful than merely falling. However, with the Starshard affixed to my forehead, my body would be in perfect balance, preventing future shameful displays. I'd awe the galaxy with flawless moves.

An old woman sat inside the shop, watching a cumbersome video display device. She wore a blue robe embroidered with complicated patterns. When she turned to face me, I stood, giving a well-practiced human smile. She walked over without uttering a word. An acrid smell smashed into my intraluminal pheromone receptors; the membrane-anchored proteins jiggled; signal-transduction cascades propagated inside my cells, threatening to alter my delicate biochemistry. I risked a cut in the mask by sealing my neck gills to prevent further invasion of her odor into my body.

"Hello, I need your services," I said.

No answer. I tried a different approach. "Isn't this great weather?" Humans who were unfriendly to each other found common ground discussing inches of precipitation.

"Uh-huh. Look, wacko, the door is open because the heat raises my blood pressure, and I have a bad heart. The sign clearly says we're closed. I don't have any money to give you for drugs either. The Pope is giving a speech." She pointed with her thumb over her shoulder. "It's live and I don't want to miss anything. So, fuck off."

I shifted to see the video display device. It sat on a low, rickety frame. On the screen, a robed male human raised his arms, provoking a coordinated cheer from the throng. Obviously, he was a revered individual. Could it be because of his headgear? I'd taken a simple approach and kept my mask bald and undecorated on top, with human mutton chops on the side. Perhaps that had been a mistake.

"Where can I buy his hat?"

She cackled. "What planet are you from?"

I froze. She'd seen through my ruse. There was no doubting her abilities.

She was eyeing me now... *suspiciously*? Upfront payment would lubricate the transaction. "There's a lost object I need to find." Her gaze followed my hand as I pulled a roll of currency from my pocket. "This is triple your price. It's very important to me."

To my right, a jar decorated with yellow ribbons sat on a table draped with a fuchsia tablecloth. I dropped the rolled currency into the jar. She licked her lips.

"I'm Madame Zozoa," she said, smiling and stretching out her right hand.

I forgot which hands clasped for greetings. A safe, universal approach was best. I grabbed her outstretched hand, turned her in a pirouette and pulled her into a hug. She was much thinner than her robe suggested. I made the hug more personable by tightening it.

"Get off!" She wiggled out of the embrace and pushed me, making me lose my balance. I grabbed the beaded curtain as I fell backwards and ripped it from the doorframe. Beads rained on my face like a rainbow meteor shower.

How dare she do this? I paid!

I controlled my anger and sat up. With widened eyes, she pointed a trembling finger at me. I felt a cool breeze and ran my fingers over my lips. My mask had ripped, exposing the lower half of my face.

"You're a demon!" Her face acquired a red hue. She started to stammer, as if her vocal box had suffered trauma.

With my identity no longer hidden, I opened and closed my neck gills in a satisfying stretch. "As you sensed earlier, I'm not from Earth. I'm blue, yes. But our bodies have similar configurations, so I doubt I'm that ugly in human eyes." The fall had also crumbled the ceramic decoys in my mouth. Without a doubt my sharp black teeth were now exposed. I raised my hands to chest level, thumbs facing up, and gave my widest smile. "I made a mistake, entering your establishment in disguise, but I thought keeping anonymous would be a good idea." I kept my smile going and remained sitting at the bottom of the steps to convince her of my friendly intentions.

She gasped for breath, clutched her chest, then jabbed her middle finger forward. This couldn't be the Macarena dance; it made no geographical sense. She grabbed the edge of the table, lost her grip, and fell to the floor, still clenching the tablecloth in her hand. Her landing was less than graceful. Luckily, her head had not impacted solid ground. Unluckily, the glass jar that held her payment, accelerated by gravity and the tablecloth's momentum, had bashed against her face.

Madame Zozoa's face contorted into a weird expression. Her eyes rolled back.

Perhaps this was what they called being in a trance. I had to try and ask my question.

"Tell me," I yelled. "Where is the Starshard?"

"*Fuuuu ...*" White foam ran out her mouth and down her cheek. I kneeled until I was inches from her face.

"Yes! What else?"

"*ufufuf—*" Her breathing accelerated, coming in rapid huffs.

I pressed my ear against her mouth. She had foul breath, but I made sacrifices for my art. "Where is the Starshard?" I repeated. Listening through the huffing and puffing for what I wanted to hear. I nodded, arranging the Fs and Us in a pattern that made sense.

When she stopped moving, I grabbed her wrist to measure her homeostasis signatures. She lived, but not comfortably. I carried her back to my ship and configured the healing chamber to human chemistry. Contacting spirits had triggered muscle failure in her heart, or perhaps it was the other way around.

Regardless, her sacrifice wouldn't go unrewarded. She was hostile at first, yet it could be argued that I had caused her health issues. But after she witnessed my Starshard enhanced moves, all would certainly be forgiven. First, I needed to consult my ship's map and complete my mission. I'd reach FUFU. I'd find the Starshard.

TROMPE-L'OEIL

T HE WOODEN BAR TOP was sticky. This would bother me for the next two or three beers, but I'd stop wondering about it afterwards.

I asked for an IPA and a shot of Jameson. The bartender was already on her way to pour my beer as I ordered it. I came here too often.

"*¿Magia, eh?*" I was practicing the conversation I'd have with López, when he got here. I glanced at my phone. No messages. I couldn't help imagining him kissing my ex-wife, Janitza, in the mouth before coming to meet with me but managed to not smash my phone on the bar top. I needed his help—nothing I'd tried had allowed me to make deals with loa.

"*Si. Magia.* But real and dangerous..." I can't believe I think magic is real. Do I? Is all magic real or just some? I shook my head. What did it matter how real things were as long as they worked? "I need a big, big favor... and it has nothing to do with

Janitza." That last part I'd leave out; it had everything to do with Janitza.

I didn't know how Agwe, the water loa in Haitian vodou, could help me get my family back, but I was ready to trade scientific thinking that had never made me happy for magic I didn't believe in.

The bartender was staring at me like a freshman after I lectured on the difference between the Michaelis constant, K_M and the dissociation constant, K_D. I smiled at her, and almost waved but stopped myself. If she saw the cuts on my palms, she'd freak out.

"Ah, shots before lunch," López said from behind me. "Getting tenure is worthy of celebration, but not that impressive, you know."

He sat next to me, then ordered a beer and shot of his own. I was surprised he was being so friendly. For him, we were probably picking up from where we left off two years ago. Years that I'd spent alone, grinding my teeth until I needed to sleep with a mouthguard.

"We used to come here all the time," he said.

"Yeah," I said. *And it's the main reason I got divorced*, I didn't say.

I got right to it. "I'm having a collection of dreams—variations of the same dream. The dreams are mostly non-linear images, but I've put them back together into something that makes sense. The physical effects are still there when I wake up."

"Huh?"

"Yeah." I drank my shot and washed it down with beer.

The bartender served López his drinks. He slammed the shot, wrinkled his face, and said, "Is that why we're drinking whisky so early?"

"It's a special occasion. I'm haunted by my dreams." I was shot-gunning sentences now. "Also, not only am I a tenured professor in biochemistry, I accomplished it three weeks before turning 50. I finally have a stable job." I laughed. The alcohol relaxed me.

I wiped the beer moustache and smile off my face. I forgot this wasn't my friend anymore.

I raised both hands and showed him the cuts on my palms. "I had these cuts after waking up from one of the dreams. I can't do anything in the dream; it's like watching myself in a movie."

"This is really worrisome," López said, his cheery attitude gone.

"I want to get some perspective and help from you," I said. "At the end of my dream a symbol forms in my mind, like water beading on a hydrophobic surface. After searching online for a few days, I know it's Agwe's vevé. Remember when you told me that you synthesized a compound that lets you invoke and speak with loa immediately, bypassing the need of spending years of worshipping or servicing or whatever?" I'm sure he did remember, not because I laughed at him, but because he now spent most of his days visiting that same house, just not to see me anymore. "You said that dreams were in fact real places we traveled to. Was it vetiver extract, from La Hispaniola or Haiti specifically? It has khusimol right? You synthesized some analog of it. I need it."

"Did you invite me here to—"

He stopped himself.

I controlled my own outburst. Did he think I invited him to drink like buddies or to just celebrate my tenure promotion after two years of not talking?

"Let's take a breath, calm down, stick to the dreams," he said.

Did he ever tell Janitza to calm down?

"Okay fine," I said. "The dreams have been happening for weeks, not every day. It's not just my hands. This morning, I woke up in blood-crusted sheets. What happens when I get a cut so deep I bleed out?"

I was desperate. "Do you know why this would happen to someone? What did I do to get Agwe's attention?"

"I've realized that the loa are parts of nature," he said and downed his drink. "No one knows why they do things. The same way we don't know why hurricanes hit the Caribbean so hard. No one needed to do something to provoke these things into occurring. Are these events predetermined, random?" He shrugged. "Just tell me your dream."

He ordered two beers.

•   •   •

We're in New Mexico. My dad's in the Army.

We're at a beach. I must be between seven and nine. My parents had taken me to the White Sands National Park a few times, but the place in the dream resembles the Caribbean, Puerto Rico, home. I'm walking along wet sand, gentle waves wash my feet. There are hundreds of people clustered in small groups, under big white umbrellas. I know them in real life; in the way you know a distant cousin that comes to Thanksgiving dinner every other year. These are people that would die as I became an adult, or their parents would die, and I, of course, would feel bad when finding out, yet it wouldn't exactly ruin my day, or push me off the career rat wheel.

I stop by a group and wait until I'm acknowledged. My right arm is snaked behind my back, with the hand cupping my left inside elbow, in that goofy way kids stand around. One of the adults yells something about how I'm Javier's kid. Everyone else nods along. I know their thoughts. They think about how Javier was going to have a baby only the other day.

They switch thinking patterns, grateful they are free from worrying about being parents. They become angry, thinking, why is this kid standing here if he isn't mine? It wasn't me who had a kid. Can he leave? I'm uncomfortable.

I stand on the shore, on the spot where the last of the waves drain into the sand. I know my mom is keeping an eye on me, but I can't see her.

A glossy, shimmering house floats on the water. It has a gable roof. The front porch is surrounded by Tuscan columns. The double doors are wrapped in barbed wire so dense it looks like wrinkled aluminum foil.

None of the adults notice. They continue talking about how hard they have it, how they are in the grind at their jobs, waiting to be on the upswing of life—grab God by the balls and the devil by the tail sort of thing.

The house has no depth. Instead of a 3D object hovering above the water, it's more like a sticker held in place. It can't be real. That's why no one notices. The panic that hadn't come when I'd seen the house rushes me all at once. I run, trying to reach a vantage point oblique enough to see behind the house, to confirm there is nothing, and decide that it's either fake or an infinitely thin slice of matter.

My mom yells for me to come back. All the other adults are yelling too.

I blink. I'm in front of the double doors; water up to my chest. I try to swim away, but the water pulls me in. The house pulls me in. I push away from the doors. Sharp metal slices my hands.

·　　·　　·

When I woke up, I knew there was a large wooden ship floating far beyond the house, despite never seeing it.

My hands were covered in dried blood. The smell in my room was like scooping up wet beach sand and breathing it in.

After washing my hands, I saw the wounds were exactly where I'd felt them in the dream.

·　　·　　·

"It's only getting worse," I told López. "Last night, I turned my back against the door—again, this was involuntary. I had to unstick myself from the bed when I woke up. My entire back felt like it was cut up." Something else had happened in the last dream that I wasn't going to share. Janitza was standing on the shore. Our daughter, Yesenia beside her, holding her hand. They were urging me to speak to Agwe and make a deal, to ask him to open the door, but nothing had been enough—all of my prayers, offerings and supplications had been met with silence.

Who had time for begging to diva gods who pretended to be deaf?

I needed a shortcut to open the door and get my family back. There was no scientific justification for me believing this, and in truth, I couldn't fully convince myself that it was real in my sober moments, but holding on to what I wanted to believe was all I had, regardless of how shaky my epistemology was.

After I got my family back, I'd quit drinking and not let alcohol ruin my life twice.

"Agwe's vevé includes his ship called Imamou. I looked it up. He's the loa of the sea right?" I asked. "I need to make a deal with him. I know what I want but not how it'll happen and it doesn't matter what he wants in return. Don't worry about the details."

"Let me check something," López said and pulled out his phone. I peeked over and saw him open Google and type *Loa dreams ti bonnanj*.

I ordered another beer, then checked my own phone. There was a text message from Yesenia.

¡Felicidades, papi!

It had taken three days for my daughter to text me back after I told her I'd been granted tenure.

I answered,

¡Gracias! It's been stressful. LOL. Celebrate with dinner soon?

I wasn't—as she'd put it—really lolling.

At least she had finally texted. If she got back to me in the next couple of weeks, we could also celebrate my birthday.

Janitza hadn't answered yet, which wasn't surprising. A year ago, she'd said her therapist recommended we stop communicating, unless it was about Yesenia. Still, she could've at least sent a congratulatory emoji.

If I spoke to her now, she'd immediately notice that I was day drinking, heavily, then give me a speech about how this ruined our marriage and how she couldn't believe I was still drinking after all that pain. If she did call, though, I'd tell her López was with me.

I ordered another beer and peeked at López's phone again. He was scrolling through a bunch of symbols, magic stuff.

"You might need protection. Agwe is a strong authority," he said.

"What I need to do is grab him by the nose and make a deal with him. He made his presence known, and I need to open that door. I looked up the foods and drinks he likes, but I don't have time to spend courting him. I need your molecule."

"You can't just take that, or—grab him by the nose." He made an indignant *pfff* noise. "Being with a loa is not transactional as you seem to think," he said. "It's a lifetime commitment of sacrifice and discipline. Loas help you help yourself. What if he asks you to do something you don't want to do. Stop drinking? Are you ready to start an ever-evolving permanent bond? Angering him will make your life worse. The door will take patience, maybe years of work. There are no shortcuts." He sipped his beer.

I thought he'd bring up my failed marriage as evidence I wasn't good enough to give offerings to a probably made-up deity and imagined punching him in the face.

I walked to the bathroom.

My legs felt tingly—no doubt drinking related—my nerves damaged by decades of alcohol abuse. I stood in front of the urinal and did a quick calculation. Ethanol had two carbons, six hydrogens, and one oxygen. Nine atoms. I had been divorced and was slowly being broken down by nine atoms. After alcohol ruined my marriage, López ruined our friendship by dating Janitza. Did he hide from her how much he drank? I closed my eyes. How much life could really be left in me?

I checked Instagram.

Janitza had posted a new story. She was in her house—our old house—standing in front of a table with a white cloth one it. On the table was a toy ouroboros, a half coconut, a white candle, and a small statue of a bearded man with Moses etched on the bottom. This was an altar to the loa Damballah, the serpent god that represented benevolence. From what I've read, Damballah was so obsessed with cleanliness that he didn't like people to get close to him when on their periods. Did that not sound sexist to anyone except me? I hit *like* on a whim. I was sure she wouldn't acknowledge me. This was the first time I had interacted with one of her posts since the divorce.

"You were in there a long time," López said.

"I was praying," I said.

He laughed, genuinely. López must have been having a great time. For a moment, I considered letting the hate go and live my life. Why not just enjoy the company of a friend? Was there a world where I could just be happy for him and Janitza?

No.

After a few more beers we switched to Guinness, since it had less alcohol and calories. In a way drinking Guinness was on path to drinking less. After a few of those, we switched to Bud Light for wrapping up the day.

It was almost dark out. "I'm sorry I was so pushy. It feels less real now," I said.

"That's because you're drunk. Tomorrow, when you're hungover and worried again, we'll go over a plan. I can't think right now. Help me drive to your house."

We walked as best we could to his car. My apartment was close but it felt like an hour; every stoplight was a puzzle you solved with one eye closed.

López sat on my couch and took off his shoes. I was happy to be in a place that had a private bathroom; I'd need it soon. He grabbed a crumpled Burger King bag from the floor. "You couldn't get a special breakfast?"

Even though it was two steps away, I barely made it to the bathroom. If alcohol was really dissolving my body away, the first thing it was solubilizing was my intestines.

I checked Instagram. Janitza had blocked me.

My heart raced. My chest tightened. I thought I was having a cardiac event, but decided it was just a panic attack when I didn't keel over with my pants around my ankles. I was dizzy now. My blood pressure probably high. What was I thinking? I didn't have any time. I could've died just now, and instead of being surrounded by loved ones, I was alone, with someone I hated drunk in the other room.

I'd let a few beers distract me. This was how it always was. Everything was important until I was drunk. I wiped myself, washed my hands, and walked out of the bathroom quickly, determined to open the door in the beach.

"I need the magic molecule now," I said. "I don't care about gods, loa, or asking for permission by dancing like an asshole or leaving food under my bed for two weeks." I gathered up my liquid courage. "The truth is, this is how I'm getting Janitza back and you can go fuck yourself."

López was fast asleep on the couch.

I shook him hard. "Please. You owe me, cabrón." But he turned to his side and snored. The cuts on my back and hands started itching like I had an oxycodone habit. I took a deep breath and took his keys out of his pockets.

López lived half an hour away. I was falling asleep behind the wheel. I bought an energy drink, and sipped it slow, so it would wake me up without triggering an aneurysm.

I was nauseated by the time I opened the door to his house.

I probably looked like a dog foaming at the mouth. My toes were curled up to the point they hurt. My hands were shaking.

He'd shown me his magic room—down the hall and to the left—countless times.

The room smelled like burnt sage. Tall jars covered in shiny, colorful sheets were arranged in rows. Each of the jars corresponded to a different loa and contained something unique inside. They were all blessed by a vodou priest or something.

In the back of the room was a short wooden table. Ceramic statues in top hats and three glass vials littered the top. The vials were the ones we commonly used in labs and were half full with a brown liquid. I opened each and smelled them. I remembered that Khusimol or at least Vetiver extracts in general, had a woody odor. The contents of all three vials smelled more or less how I expected. I was pretty sure none of these compounds were particularly toxic, so I decided I'd just drink all three.

With one of the vials on my lips, a loa jar—nearly out of my field of view—shook in place. I was startled and dropped the vials. They shattered. I stared at the jar for a few seconds, straining my ears; it stayed still.

Tears welled up in my eyes, my lips quivered, but instead of collapsing on the floor, decades of lab training and problem-solving kicked in. I ran to the kitchen, grabbed some paper towels and a Ziploc bag. If I could soak up the liquid, I'd extract the molecules from the paper towel with an organic solvent—maybe methanol—then purify and structurally characterize them using nuclear magnetic resonance and X-ray crystallography. I'd synthesize these molecules from scratch if I had to.

Back in the magic room, the floor was covered in cold water that reached my ankles. The few milliliters of molecules were lost, infinitely diluted.

It smelled like brine. I looked down and saw that I had urinated myself. When had this happened? Was this real?

My tongue felt smooth, as if coated in snail slime. I didn't have a specific memory in which I had drunk the vial contents. Had I?

When I looked up, a black man with green eyes stood in the middle of the room, right where I had dropped the vials. He was naked, with a conch hanging around his neck, held by thin frayed rope. He tapped his nose—as if to say, here it is—and smiled.

"What?" I asked, dazed.

"Mwen se Agwe, and I'll give you what you want for a fair trade," he said.

I turned to run away.

The door from my dreams stood in front of me. It shuddered. The barbed wire unwound like a spool of string and disappeared.

The door opened. Janitza and Yesenia sat at a dinner table. It was the same table I'd bought years ago. They were laughing. From out of view, I walked into the scene—a version of me that weighed at least 30 pounds less. This me probably slept restfully through the night, no restless leg syndrome, and without his body rejecting all the booze he drank.

He/I bent down and kissed Janitza on the forehead. She smiled without showing teeth, like a schoolgirl in love for the first time.

The hairs on my arm stood up. I was excited—violently anxious to jump through that door, choke my other self to death, and take his place. My muscles tensed, but Agwe placed his hand on my shoulder and held me in place.

"Is this what you want?" Agwe asked.

I nodded but didn't turn to face him in case the scene in front of me disappeared when I stopped looking. "Whatever you want in return. I fully believe now," I said.

"Those words will become heavier with time. Belief hurts more than you think," he said and laughed.

"I don't care," I said.

He passed me the conch and said, "Drink."

I brought it up to my lips. The liquid inside smelled like sweet rum, Caribbean aguardiente. I drank, at first worried about what the alcohol would do to me, but then I started feeling better, stronger.

I drank faster without taking a moment to breathe.

We were on the deck of an old, creaking ship. It was Immamou. Salt water splashed around us. We floated in front of the door from my dreams. Beyond the door, I saw myself—me as I am now—with Janitza, and Yesenia happy. I started walking to the door. The more steps I took, the closer the ship moved—I wouldn't need to walk on water.

Agwe's hand rested on my shoulder again—this time wet and chilly.

My eyes burned with the cold. Tears froze on my cheeks. Agwe whispered, "After a taste of reward comes a bit of service."

THE ORGANOMETALLIC GOD

AFTER SARA'S FLESH dissolved away, only a brittle blood-streaked skeleton, held together by Caribbean magic and covered with clumps of dried fat, remained. The strong smell of pine trees outside the cabin gradually disappeared as if the vegetation had uprooted itself and fled after espying through the windows what she'd become. The log cabin where she'd gone for her honeymoon—a place full of fond memories—was now her prison. She couldn't move, but her mind reeled, filled with new knowledge, a hidden truth: this limbo between life and death confirmed the supernatural existed.

She'd suffered much already, struggling against chronic disease for years to only then lose most of her physical self to a supposed cure, but the fear of loss lingered, transforming into the terror of losing her identity, the last bastion in her defeated territory. She could feel her awareness, the thing that made her who she was, sifting through her calcified fingers like dry sand.

Small things she'd enjoyed when alive felt alien. What kind of ice cream had been her favorite? Now that she had no tongue, she wondered how humans didn't think it strange to have a slab of wet flesh moving ceaselessly inside their mouths, swirling saliva and bacteria. Had she stopped thinking of herself as human?

She'd grown up in a religious home, a flat-roofed cement house in San Juan, but her parents' piousness had never appealed to her. She had prayed with her mouth to appease her mother but never with her heart, a fact that hadn't changed even after the cancer diagnosis, nor when the doctors said there was nothing they could do to help. Finally, desperation and darkness had won out. Now, for the first time in her life, Sara concentrated and begged God to save her, to stop her soul from fragmenting as her body had. Would her mother be proud or disappointed that she gave in only when presented with undeniable evidence?

She imagined her mother's voice, begging, *no seas como Santo Tomás el incrédulo, hija. Abre los ojos y ve al Señor.*

Yet, she had no eyes.

She felt a faint graze as Marcos ran his fingers over her exposed clavicle. They had been married for so long that by merely hearing how sharply his boots tapped the ground, she could tell he was excited, as if her flesh dissolving was part of his plan and not a freak accident.

Despite the lack of nerve endings on her skeleton, anxiety accumulated in her bones like an imprisoned electric charge. She tried to stand from her chair and take a few steps to relieve the restless leg syndrome that had developed in her advanced age. Instead, she remained still; the last of her cartilage and sinews floated away like burning ash.

She mustered all her concentration again, imagining her entire being flying upwards to the sky, screaming in her mind for mercy, for the peace promised after death in the few holy texts she was vaguely familiar with, yet God didn't answer.

Marcos paced away, sat in the chair across from her, and knitted his brow, studying her like an unsolvable puzzle, a lab specimen. She tried to rotate her skull, to look away, and show her disapproval but failed. She had no stomach to hold nausea, or scalp to lose hair from, or a biological clock counting down how much life was left in her, but this degrading state wasn't better than the prospect of dying from cancer. The uncertainty of how she was alive without flesh, the slipping of her senses, her mind losing its built-in persona, all made the idea of death a blessing.

In the beginning of her sickness, despite her body being infested with rapidly multiplying masses of tumor tissue, it had fallen on her to comfort Marcos when she'd become sick—sacrificing most of what little energy she had—and force him to confront reality: death was unescapable, axiomatic.

It hadn't worked. Marcos had spent every ounce of energy trying to keep her alive, and in a way succeeded. There were many failures in the beginning; mounds of innocent mice poisoned by Marcos's chemical concoctions. But, playing god in the lab was not enough and instead of accepting her fate, he turned to witchcraft, enhancing science with Santería—chants and blood sacrifices hand in hand with proton spins and mass fragmentation patterns, actions lacking both sanity and scientific rigor.

When he told her that he'd found the molecule that cured cancer in mice, it was too late to test in humans; Sara's tumors had spread like famished parasites. He'd promised everything would be all right after she drank the experimental elixir, that he was finally in control of the disease, that he would never leave her side. Participating in his experiments was madness, but the pain in his eyes mirrored that in her body. In a last effort to alleviate both of their agonies, she drank—she would die soon enough, regardless.

The weight of pain becomes lighter when carried by two, he said frequently, back when they were naïve and self-assured—

when her body slipped into the initial stages of disease, before his love mutated into hubris.

He pulled a glass vial from his shirt pocket, unscrewed the cap, then brought the vial up to his nose and winced. Sara remembered the atrocious smell, yet she could no longer summon up the experience of scents.

"Together forever," he said, and drank.

A panicking heat mixed in with the electric itch coating her body, energizing her rigid limbs.

She wondered how her sense of sight still worked after seeing her eyeballs fall out of her face. Another question that would probably never be answered. Magic had given her a clear demonstration of its existence, not a description of its mechanism of action. *Please God. Please Allah. Anyone, anywhere. Help me. I'm scared.*

Silence. Pain.

Marcos relaxed in his chair. "Science failed me, but I won't fail you. This isn't a cure. I lied. I've conquered Santería more than anyone can understand." He sighed, then smiled, and continued: "I pretended to make a deal with Eleguá, the master of the spiritual crossroads, a trickster god. I was able to deceive him instead."

Why did tricking a god necessitate lying to her? Anger caused by betrayal and violated trust banged at her rib cage like a tortured specter. Her name vanished from her mind, substituted by images of the deception he'd played, the frustration of their 40-year marriage. She could not grasp exactly what fed her fury, but it was the only thing left. She held onto it, telling herself it made her human—the hot simmer of hatred in place where her heart should be.

He took a deep breath, growled like a wild animal and started to sing. "*Eleguá, señor de los caminos, primero de los Orishas, te hemos domado.*" His skin tinged yellow, wrinkled, then cracked in the span of a few seconds, as her own had after drinking his elixir. "Sara, after your consciousness leaves your body, sing the following words to release me from my own skeleton. He is tamed!"

"Abre para nosotros—"

His mouth kept moving, but Sara was unable to hear. Her vision dimmed as Marcos' skin started to crumble off his body. He sat back into his chair and smirked.

She had no interest in cooperating this time, and his confession had given her an idea. If Santería worked for him, then it might work for her. She'd never believed in supernatural phenomena, yet now knew it to be true. Marcos had been faithless his entire life, and somehow still found a deity that listened to petty men who fantasized with wielding absolute control over life and death. If Marcos could offer something the spirits wanted, then so could she.

Instead of praying, she made her own deal. Her freedom, for whatever the other party wanted in exchange, as long as she was able to remain herself, a person who would recognize her mother if she smiled from Heaven in approval. She focused her intention, like a beam shooting from her head, piercing realities, willing it to reach Eleguá's path.

After going completely blind and deaf, her soul plunged into darkness, anger dissipating. The room where her husband waited vanished as if it had never existed. Whatever Marcos thought his singing had triggered wasn't going to keep them together after death. She would not sing for his liberation.

Their cabin was deep in the woods; their presence there unknown to everyone they knew.

Floating in the darkness, she imagined him as an immobile skeleton and reveled in how much he deserved to sit and think about his failure at both mastering science and fooling the gods, to regret lying to her. No one would come to sing and release his soul. He'd live on like a statue until he crumbled to dust, powerless, God of nothing.

•   •   •

A pair of hands covered in a grainy material pulled Sara out of the darkness and into a blinding light. Sadness lingered for a few moments until it, along with its source, disappeared from her mind, forgotten. Happiness filled her as she remembered marrying Eleguá, a natural act when dealing with the Orishas. Soft, unintelligible chanting surrounded her, increasing in volume at the pace of a slow crescendo. A warm, sage-scented breeze blew away her pain, leaving her heavy and numb, sleepy but restless. She tasted blood and heard the laughter of spirits.

BUTTER ME UP AND FLOAT ME SIDEWAYS

SOON AFTER PLANET LIPIDIA'S DISCOVERY, the aquatic sport of brine racing had been developed with excitement—and not safety—in mind. For many on Earth, it would become the new must-watch sporting event of the week, but for Theodore it was the only way to find justice after being arrested, unfairly convicted of involuntary manslaughter, and sent off-planet to serve a six-year prison sentence.

To be fair, he *had known* that preparing fat-burning enzyme cocktails in a dirty university laboratory was not the safest way to start a weight loss business, but you could sell anything online, and postdoctoral salaries in academia flirted dangerously close to the poverty line.

The race would be full of surprises. But Theo had an advantage. He had a PhD in biochemistry and knew all about how fat worked: how the second law of thermodynamics described the hydrophobic effect, the angle between carbon and hydrogen atoms in a sp3 tetrahedral arrangement, and the contribution an aqueous solvent's ionic strength played in hydrophobic interactions.

"Welcome to the first ever annual brine race!" the announcer declared from a central platform floating in the middle of what looked like a circular lake. "Planetary revolutions work differently here on Lipidia. Instead of boring the audience and viewers back home with scientific details, I'll just give you the skinny. On Earth, we'll get a total of one race every week. Tell me that isn't fatty fat fantastic!" The glitter around her eyes glimmered bright purple. The sun rays bounced off her red shiny dress like kids in a bouncy house.

Theodore was dropped off by boat to his own platform. A barrel full to the brim with steaming lard and a scuba tank were already waiting for him. He tottered as he climbed onto the platform, but managed to find his balance. If he fell into the lake without protection, they'd pull him out drier and saltier than beef jerky, if they bothered to pull him out at all. He took a deep breath to calm his nerves, zipped down his oversized orange jumpsuit, then took off his sweat stained t-shirt and pulled down his soiled boxers before standing straight and proud in the blue Speedo he'd spent months saving for. The jumper and boxer shorts, in a pile beside his scuba tank, were the only items given to him after arriving at Lipidia's prison.

His uniform had made his body itch every second of every day, enough to keep him up at night. His body was covered in scratch marks. The clothes had already been well-stained—from sweat, among other things—when he'd received his uniform.

He shivered, from both the breeze and the sight of what he had just been wearing. Whatever happened in the race, he promised himself he'd be carried on the shoulders of fans to receive his freedom—as prize for winning first place—or zipped up in a black bag destined to the prison furnace. Even after being released, it'd be hard for him, as an ex-con, to find a job, especially in drug development, but there were other ways to build legacies. For example, he'd win the first ever brine race and become famous.

Theodore scooped some of the warm lard with his hands, then smeared it across his body, careful not to run his hands too many times over the same area and end up removing the coat. He covered every inch of his skin, making sure the fat went in between his toes, and inside his Speedo, deep in his ass crack. The audience giggled, but he required perfect hydrophobicity.

The best method for coating oneself in fat had been debated among sports experts and would no doubt be fed by superstition and pseudoscience in the future. Recorded podcasts between self-appointed journalists and Wikipedia Warriors had been sent up to Lipidia, where prisoners could listen and re-listen while waiting for an epiphany.

Some racers swiped the fat from side to side, others dropped a dollop of melted lard on their shaved heads and dragged it down as if rolling on a liquid condom. Finally, the racers strapped on their scuba tanks and adjusted the circular mask over their nose and mouths.

"Please appreciate the different strategies for preparation," the announcer said, then looked up at the hovering drones. "I'm not an expert in hydrodynamics—whatever those are—but I'd say the more buttered up they are the better!"

Theo was confident. His thesis work had been on the effect of cholesterol content on the stiffness of cell membranes. His knowledge on the partition coefficients of non-polar molecules with water was finally going to become useful. He dipped his buttered-up finger into the lake and found that the liquid pushed back.

Colloquially, the liquid portions on planet Lipidia were said to be made of water, but this was not so. The liquid was a solvent that had a much higher solubility limit for salt, thus increasing its overall ionic strength or "saltiness," its hate for fat molecules, and its toxicity. Despite these dangers, brine racing found little opposition from the political class, and the prisoners here didn't get a vote.

The announcer took a deep breath. "Racers, get ready to *brrriine!*"

The crowd cheered.

Theodore barely heard the gunshot signaling the beginning of the race. His goggles slipped through his fingers and then onto his forehead before he finally got them on. He jumped into the liquid that wasn't water and swam as hard as he could. Most racers were in front of him. The rush of fluid and the thundering of his own heartbeat drowned out the instructions, encouragement, and cursing coming from the crowd. Theodore swam like a frog, sliding off the surface like a flicked ping-pong ball. The guy in the lead swam like a child slapping at the water, bopping up and down while moving forward. Despite the staggering number of inmates in Lipidia prison, only ten swam per race. This way, the river wasn't crowded, and there could be weekly heats with fresh inmates to entertain viewers. Which was especially important, since only the ultra-rich could afford to come see the races live, providing a steady stream of income for the warden.

A few hundred yards south, the entry tube was screwed in place atop a waterfall that, in turn fed into the Eastern Jail River, a slow-moving river that happened to be the deepest on the planet. To reach the river safely, racers needed to enter the tube and slide down, sharing a stream that was wide enough for only two people side by side. The tube's design aimed at promoting patience and a sense of community among prisoners.

Theo found himself to the right of an inmate with spider leg tattoos stretching down his temples. Despite the shaved head and blob of fat on his face, he recognized Cono, with whom he shared kitchen duty most weeks, where Theo was tasked with chipping away frozen chicken wings from a frozen solid clump the size of his head—an exercise the guards claimed helped build character—that had formed from too many freeze/thaw cycles on their way from Earth.

Cono smiled through his mask. Theo smiled back.

They entered the tube.

"Theo, let's team up until the end," Cono yelled over the sound of the water. "Whoa. The echo in here is nuts."

"Licorice formation?" Theo asked.

Cono nodded. The licorice formation had been proposed by a sports medicine expert Theo had met in grad school, who'd promised her strategy led to the best combination of efficiency and endurance.

They exited the tube. Palm trees were scattered along the riverbank.

Theo looked back and said, "I think I'm a bit faster. I'll take the front first." Theo swam forward, and when Cono was far enough behind him to be the size of a thumb, Theo swam left and slowed down. Cono came up on his right side and sped up, then Theo swam right and accelerated and Cono swam left. They outlined what surely looked like an ellipse from above. The licorice formation was supposed to allow fluidity, with the racers swimming around in an intertwining fashion while giving both racers a few seconds to rest. The idea was to trap opponents inside the ellipse and simultaneously attack and push them to the riverbank. From the looks of it, Theo could outswim Cono when the time came.

Two swimmers were catching up with them.

"Let us pass, ladies, and we won't hurt you," one of them yelled.

Cono decelerated to let both racers pass and positioned himself behind them. They were inside the licorice trap.

The next turn in the river was one of the tightest in the race. To make matters worse, large boulders stuck out where the water was shallow. "Dead Man's Curve," as the media had named it, was a bad place to smash into at the speeds they were traveling. And if Theo's plan worked, he'd send these two guys there.

He rotated 180 degrees and rushed towards the two racers—an action possible only because he'd been slowing down for a while. The gap between them started closing fast. A few dozen yards away, one of the racers rotated upside down, riding on his greased-up back. The other racer laid on top of him, belly to belly, Speedo to Speedo. Both racers straightened their arms, fists facing forward: the butter beam. Theo had heard interviews where a retired boxer had mused about the effectiveness of the butter beam, and had no interest in experiencing it in real life.

Theo took a deep breath—which he didn't need since he had a scuba tank—and swam downwards. If he managed to dip below his opponents, he'd pass underneath them, come out the other side, and help them into the rocks. Except this super salty liquid really didn't like fat, so instead of going deep enough, he was pushed upwards, broke through the surface, and spent a half second twirling in the air before landing on his opponents in a Speedo to Speedo to Speedo arrangement.

"Shit!" one of them said.

Theo didn't wait. He grabbed the mask of the guy below him and tore it off.

"Help!"

Theo slipped off the jumble of arms and legs, spun on his belly like a top, and found himself face to face with Cono.

"We did it, man!" Theo said.

"Sorry," Cono said, avoiding eye contact.

"No! We can still work together!" Theo pleaded.

Cono grabbed at Theo's head, but his hands slipped. Theo kicked hard, waiting for an opening to yank Cono's mask off. Cono clasped Theo's elbows, holding on like a crab on steroids, then turned Theo sideways. Unable to kick in the water, Theo was at Cono's mercy.

"Look behind you. I can't take being here anymore. You can win next time! I'm sorry!" Cono yelled. He released Theo and swam left.

Theo didn't spend time screaming back at Cono that prison wasn't a stroll in the park for him either. He turned to see the motionless bodies of the two other racers floating among the rocks.

He was traveling too fast to stop himself, so he made a split-second calculation, taking into account his mass and speed, and decided to take a sharp right turn, then rotated until his tank was pointing toward the riverbank.

Boom!

Theo's tank exploded. His body skittered across the ground like a stone skipping across a pond. He sat up, dazed, but luckily all his limbs worked. He was covered in dried-out palms from a nearby tree, but he didn't remove them to avoid scraping off any more fat.

"Nice outfit!"

A group of racers laughed as they passed him. He took off his tank, but kept the mask and hoses attached to it, then ran along the shore, chasing after the swimmers. But even if he caught up with them, Cono was too far ahead.

Instead of giving up, he thought of the mashed potatoes they had for lunch the day before, and ran faster.

The blob of racers reached the second waterfall. The exit tube was the only way down. They battled, nearly clogging the tube like a lifetime of eating bacon cheeseburgers does an artery. The racers made it through before Theo could jump into the water and steal a scuba tank.

He stood now at the top of the waterfall, watching the racers travel through the tube like chunks of cholesterol.

Defeated.

In the distance he saw a lone dot, Cono, traveling toward a huge banner with the word *Freedom* written on it—the finish line!

Theo sat on the ground and leaned against a huge boulder with his legs hanging over the edge. The boulder—big enough to be composed of several thousand chicken wings—shifted a bit and he leaned in with it. He grew tired as the adrenaline wore off.

The Itch!

Theo jumped to a standing position and pulled out crumbled leaves from his Speedo, then scratched like a flea-ridden ape. He remembered how his prison uniform was made of the itchiest fabric in the known galaxy. The itch and the prison food were enough to make dying while trying to win worth it. He nearly jumped from the edge, to either his death or the tiniest chance of winning, when he had an idea. The only tools around him were any bits of nature within reach, his coating of fat, and his overrated advanced degree. But that was enough. Now that he was far from the commotion, he heard the drones hovering above him. He looked up and gave them a thumbs up. Why not give them a show? He was about to try something worth talking about, after all.

The plan was simple: jump into the water, go deep, and pop out like a cork flying off a pressurized bottle of champagne. He lifted the boulder he'd been leaning against and hugged it close to his chest. It had to be close to 100 pounds. Even better. He took a deep breath and jumped off the cliff, hoping the river was as deep as it looked.

After the initial splash, his surroundings went dark. Pain shot up his wrists as he gripped the boulder.

Thud!

He'd reached the bottom. His ears popped and his body shook from the repulsive force of the liquid around him. He started to blow air out and prepared to kick; hopefully he'd surface at an angle and not shoot straight up.

He let go of the boulder.

The goggles flew off his face. Instead of breaking the surface with the grace of a humpback whale leaping out of the water, he flew like a catapulted ragdoll, trying to curl into a ball and protecting his neck so it wouldn't snap. The trees sped backwards.

No! He was speeding forward!

The image of a spider coated in fat blurred by.

"Sorry!" he yelled and broke through the freedom banner.

He'd broken his leg after splashing into the water, but he'd won. Before losing consciousness, he wondered if chickens could fly.

•   •   •

Theo was shipped back home and moved back into this mom's house, unable to get a job. At least, the money from the interviews had helped pay for some food. He enjoyed his fifteen minutes of fame to the fullest. The cast on his leg got signed by Michael Jordan, Tom Brady, and Michael Phelps.

The media also took off with the race's footage, playing the video of him jumping off the cliff while hugging a rock every single day for a week.

The move was initially named pulling a Theo. The deeper a swimmer sank into the river, the faster they shot up to the surface; a slingshot effect as it were, facilitated by the entropic push of hydrophilic molecules against the swimmer's fat coating. Of course, it was risky. Plummeting too deep and navigating submerged obstacles at high speed were both dangerous, never mind the possibility of flying too high before landing on the water a second time. Many more racers tried it over the years, with a near zero success rate. Decades later, this move was referred to as Theo's Gambit.

Neither entry nor exit tubes were ever replaced with wider versions to discourage racers from trying this trick— the prison had a tight budget.

DROWNED IN MINDFULNESS

T HE WALL IS SENTIENT and has a long memory; it stretches to either side, seemingly into infinity.

The wall allows me to write on its surface, yet I am only rewarded when I communicate scientific truths, and if I try to repeat myself, the pleasure I get decreases. I have all the writing space I could need, but the wall only wants new science.

There have been others here before me. Imagine my surprise when I saw Boltzmann's equation: $S = k_b \ln W$ in red, fist-sized letters across the wall.

Soon after, I learned that everyone, and everything, becomes part of the wall.

The wall motivates me to narrate every bit of information I can muster. Unfortunately, I'm currently out of ideas.

But I am not completely selfish. I'll describe to you my surroundings and the details of my death. After all, what if you die and end up here? I abandoned you, but you're still my daughter. And if you end up here, it will help to have notes from someone you trusted.

Sharing will also give me time to think of something new I can trade with the wall.

•   •   •

I'd prefer you found out how to write on the wall from me and not personal experience. The woman who taught me must've been around your age when she died. Like me, she was also naked, her body gray with decay.

The sounds escaping her mouth were barely human, as if something else howled from within her, clawing up her insides to use her throat as a megaphone.

From a few snippets I'd read, she was a PhD student in biochemistry and had accidentally overdosed on heroin. I, meanwhile, knew exactly what drinking that much D_2O would do to me. We were similar, yet different. Am I in a wing of hell that specializes in scientists who died by suicide? That would explain why this place isn't thronging with the damned.

I kept my distance as she scrawled on the wall, hiding behind one of the sticky tar-coated trees that emerged from the ground when one wasn't looking. The black leaves rotated toward me on their limp branches, like sentient touch-me-nots that here in the afterlife finally cast off their shyness. I was still a new arrival back then and out of cautiousness, avoided touching them.

In a blink of an eye, in one of those moments where my gaze settled on sandy distances away from the wall, the tree disappeared.

The woman's dedication to her story was impressive. To her left was what looked like miles of text she'd written. Her crying, the screams of pain, blended into my senses the same way the grainy ground scratched the spaces between my toes.

Seconds after she stopped writing, a strange feeling came up from my feet and concentrated in my forehead, like a homunculus telling me to look away and leave. The discomfort was like staring into the eyes of a terminally ill loved one after saying your goodbyes and crying by their bedside. Awkwardness. What was there left to say? One of us will continue living and the other one will not.

As I walked away, the screams escaping the young woman grew louder, despite my increasing distance. A low humming sound rose from the ground and a wave of heat hit the back of my neck. Curiosity and apprehension made me turn. The wall surrounding her had become... 'liquid' is the only word that comes to mind. Both of her arms were trapped, sucked into the wall, which was melting in place, an air-suspended liquid. The scene teased me into thinking physics worked differently here.

She was elbow deep in the viscous ripples when her body started to melt as though her heart was pumping liquid wall into her. Her knees bent the wrong way, her hips tilted at an impossible angle, sending her ribcage to rest on her waist, yet her feet remained grounded.

As she slumped, waist deep in the wall, her head fell backwards, like the hood of a jacket being shrugged off. The upside-down twisted smile I saw on her bubbling face forced my eyes closed. I ran away. This time, I didn't turn back.

I am only going to share what I noticed next for the sake of being thorough. Who can know what details are important to write or leave out?

As I ran from the scene, I noticed I had an erection; not caused by the sight of the naked woman since I had been looking at her for a while. The wall had somehow triggered that effect. When I was done running, I sat on the dusty ground and breathed hard until I realized I wasn't out of breath—which made sense, since I was dead.

When I found enough courage to go back to the wall, I cautiously tapped its cool, solid surface to see if it would try to consume me too, but nothing happened.

She had written her story in blood, and without knowing it, she'd taught me how to write mine. I bit my thumb until blood dripped down to my wrist. There was no pain.

I was never fond of writing when alive, but the delicious tickling I was getting in exchange for my words was too good to ignore.

•   •   •

There are more phenomena worthy of mention. Serpentine creatures curl and coil with each other in the gray sky. If I stare for too long at their black, iridescent scales, they notice me, lock their gazes with mine—bright red eyes so deep that it feels like my blood has thickened, and my heart is struggling to pump viscous muck through my veins. Although that sensation could be something I dragged from life into death. My cause of death was undoubtedly some sort of cardiac event. And because of my age, I'm sure there weren't any further inquiries.

But I assure you, I took my own life. If I'm correct, the tool I used to end myself was never detected by the doctors.

I was sick of the suffering that comes hand-in-hand with consciousness, the bug sullying the minds of lifeforms naïve enough to evolve it.

I am sure that by now, the funeral came and went. I wonder if people cried, or eulogized me as a good, if eccentric, person. Were my past accomplishments celebrated? Or perhaps my future scientific contributions also mourned now that I would never get to them?

Wait. I just had an idea. The pleasure the wall gives me feels like having an orgasm pass into my thumb, then spreading into my entire body, a very concrete sensation, which means it probably has a biological component. Bioelectrical sensations can be propagated by the influx or efflux of ions through transmembrane proteins called ion channels. This transfer of ions can change the resting potential of—

That felt good. Nowhere near to the best ones, but I'm satisfied for now, so let's continue.

The wall is pristine—a white so brilliant that I always squint when looking at it—while the ground is black, with the consistency of finely powdered limestone. A hazard if I were alive and cared about the health of my lungs.

There are also no sounds or any indications as to what could be on the other side of the wall. At first, I thought this place was purgatory and beyond the wall was hell, or perhaps heaven, and I was simply waiting for my number to come up. But I've come to think of a meaningful afterlife as a farce, of demons and angels as mere human inventions.

Imagine living your entire life waiting to start 'living' after you die. Ridiculous.

How many religions existed that I knew nothing about? This wall could be foretold by one of them. Maybe no religion got it right, and the white wall sat here, wondering why we invented bearded men who governed the sky when only it peered through the cosmos.

Honestly, who cares? I am dead and I am here. The wall's rewards are enough to keep me going.

But I am not immune from guilt, and I regret whatever pain my dying caused you. Your mother and I always struggled with how to make you comfortable at every moment. I remember when you skipped nearly all the classes during your first semester in college, hiding in the dorm room while we remained unaware for months. The anxiety over being outside, on a strange campus, with strangers who walked around reciting knowledge you had yet to learn, was too much to handle. We were suspicious you were skipping some classes but decided that breathing down your neck would be invasive. Adults need to learn to make decisions on their own. Only when you got kicked out did we realize our error in judgment.

When you became pregnant and glowed with never-ending happiness, I knew I could go in peace. Yet, I remained paranoid. What if you had issues with the pregnancy and something unexpected and horrible happened, leading you to seclude yourself and reverting to the habits of your teenage years, unwilling to leave the house until the acne disappeared?

Except now, the hesitation to participate in society would have worse consequences than failing out of college. So, I wanted to keep an eye on you and came up with what I thought was a very clever idea. I could die, but I needed to die slowly, and retain the ability to reverse the process if needed.

I drank D_2O, deuterium oxide, which you'll probably recognize by its common name, heavy water. Compared to regular water or H_2O, heavy water is more viscous, has a higher boiling point, and ultimately is not suitable for maintaining life. But there's a catch; one drink won't kill. In my case, it took weeks of near-constant consumption. Heavy water is still similar enough to water, plus the deuterium atoms can be exchanged for protons since the bonds to oxygen are labile, leading to the formation of the hybrid molecule HDO. It's because of the electronegativity of oxygen that these bonds can break and re-form...

That felt good. Let me find more.

Two atoms bonded together can be imagined as being connected by vibrating springs. If an atom is replaced by a heavier one, then more energy is needed to make the spring vibrate, and even more can make one atom pop off the other.

I can feel it flowing into me. I'm trying to push it back so it accumulates and then rushes into me all at once.

Thinking of atoms in this way led to the discovery of what we call kinetic isotope effect. To show this experimentally, you'd measure the abstraction rate of a deuteron or protium from a molecule and then—

Sorry. My knees gave out after the rush. I spent several moments dazed on the floor in sweet bliss.

But I'm back now.

I wonder what will happen when all the knowledge I have is written on the walls, when the entirety of my scientific career, hobbies, odds and ends are finally laid out and the only thing that's left is an empty husk, a book cover with spine and front and back boards, but with no pages sewn in.

This is a problem for later. And after that big one I just experienced, I'll be satisfied for a while and can continue with what I'm sure you really want to know: the *why* of my death.

•   •   •

I was sitting in my office, experiencing the happiest moment a man in my position could hope for, when I decided to end my life.

In the span of a few minutes, the most prestigious scientific journal in my field accepted the manuscript I had submitted a year before, and you texted me that you were finally pregnant. If your mother had still been alive, she would've said that these two events were more than mere coincidence; indeed, it was an example of synchronicity, the universe trying to tell me something. This kind of mystical thinking felt too ungrounded for me to buy into. My scientific training had suffocated any curiosity regarding supernatural phenomena. Occurrences in our world were either explicable or not explicable *yet*.

After the veil had been lifted, any solved mysteries would be detailed following the rules of the natural world.

How could we justify the existence of supernaturalism if it had yet to take credit for a single known phenomenon? Did one make positive claims about a power that had accomplished nothing?

Even this place, this wall I'm using to write to you, can be eventually demystified by science. The wall feels cool and smooth under my bleeding thumb. Why should I then conclude it's made of magic and not atoms? Why not assume that my body is still composed of mostly water and carbon-based organic molecules, that the enzymes that catalyze chemical reactions in my body had the same biochemical properties in this place, the same turnover rate, the same melting temperature. Am I to doubt that hexokinase phosphorylates glucose in the first step of glycolysis just because I am in this hell? Should I—

I wish you could have felt it. The pleasure spread through my entire body like food coloring in warm water. I should've saved that for later and not spent it so soon after the previous one.

Let's get back to my story; thinking about wasting pleasure gives me anxiety.

I did love your mother, so I tried to meet her beliefs halfway. At least, if I were flexible about viewing things her way, we would have had more things to do together. She was mindful of how I felt and suggested an activity that had some scientific justification. So, months before I received that awesome email and your text, when her cancer first appeared, we started meditating.

As we meditated, we learned about how thoughts rule our lives if we let them, and other concepts that I don't pretend to understand fully. As I see it, meditation promises to liberate you from the suffering of letting thoughts run amok in your head. For example, how necessary is it to practice a fight with your spouse dozens of times before the actual encounter? What if you never end up fighting in the end? Did you suffer for nothing? It's hard to imagine answering no to this last question. You indeed suffered because of something that isn't and—even worse—might never be real. Is this not idiocy?

I never managed to reach an enlightened state in which I could extinguish the suffering that was only 'in my head.' But I didn't see *no* effect either.

What happened to me was much worse. I couldn't be happy anymore, or at least enjoy happy moments in earnest. At meditation practice, we learned that the self, as in one-self, or what most people think of themselves—the little person who lives behind your eyes, the thinker—is an illusion. That there is no thinker in your head, but instead, thoughts simply *arise* in consciousness. I'm aware of how confusing this sounds. Now, we could dig deeper and ask what it means to be aware. But we won't.

I can give you a concrete example. I am happy that you will finally become a mother after trying for years. But if consciousness is the substrate for pain and suffering, how happy should I really be that you're bringing another conscious being into existence? Am I a hypocrite? How do I resolve this conflict? You see, at this point I am already lost in thought, suffering in my head. Alone. Not even death could save me.

As I absorbed these lessons, my mind did indeed change. My emotions broke. Things I loved, that made me happy, became reflections of thoughts that I now knew to be illusions. Of course, the bad emotions weren't that easy to eliminate. In fact, the intensity of my suffering doubled, as if sadness filled the vacuum left by my now-lost happiness. Some researchers categorize these symptoms into what they call the affective domain, but I'm a chemist and have no idea—or care—what that means.

Meditation was promised to me as a miracle cure. Instead, it delivered all the side effects and none of the therapeutic benefits. In some sense, it was a perfect poison.

And all this negativity and suffering came from the fact that we have consciousness, and we are powerless to help ourselves. What short of the power of a god could remove this curse from humanity?

So, when I opened the email congratulating me on my new paper and received the text from you telling me I was going to be a grandfather, I experienced a moment of utter joy, then the feeling vanished. I slammed my fists on my desk and stood from my chair. Where had my fucking happiness gone? A sense of vertigo swam in my head, like I was trying to stand on billiard balls and balance myself to keep from falling. The desk, bookshelf, and floor took a soft glow resembling yellow, fluorescent molecules manifesting themselves millimeters deep in the matter, emitting photons that reached my eyes and told my brain that I was indeed seeing the impossible. The yellow glow spread to the floor and ceiling, the brightness oscillated from too dim to see to a glow so intense, I had to close my eyes—and I saw it still, through my eyelids. The color seemed warm and welcoming. Everything in my office was soaked in the glow, except my body and clothes. I did not belong to it. After shaking my head and blinking a few times, the color disappeared and left me alone. I took a deep breath and shuffled out of the office and into my lab.

It was a Monday afternoon, so most people were working on the benches or typing away at their computers. At first glance, things looked normal, but after a few seconds, the world was different. My students all looked like their skins were coated with oily pastels, as if an artist had tried to rush and give life to the lifeless, painting skin and lips and makeup on mannequins to give them a sense of being real while they toiled away at mindless duties that didn't matter, following thoughts that didn't come from a thinker inside their heads, but instead were products of chemical collisions in their brains, coincidences of entropy.

They were doing their best to pursue the lab's mission. My mission. A mission that came from a person who knew thoughts were a phenomenon to be witnessed and not created.

I squeezed my hands, contemplated my life, and whimpered. I said "excuse me" or something else to that effect, grabbed a one-liter bottle of D_2O—no one even paid attention to me— then rushed back to my office. I uncapped, sniffed at the odorless liquid, and took the first sip of the end of my life. Nothing mattered. There was no hope. Consciousness was the true burden. And I would end mine.

I am relieved I finally shared this with you.

•　　•　　•

I have been here so long, I've gone from talking to myself to changing the voices when I address a point I had previously made, as if I were composed of different people, each with their own opinions.

Everything is broken now. I can write the most elaborate equation or chemical reaction scheme I can think of and the fucking wall doesn't even give me a tickle. Are my spiritual balls empty?

I tried to rewrite old ideas, trying to enjoy myself even a minuscule amount, but my blood beaded on the wall and fell to the ground, rejected. No pleasure, but enough pain to make me cry, filling me with a dread so strong I have no memory of ever feeling anything similar. Not even when I was alive.

There must be something I can do.

•   •   •

For the last few weeks—at least, I think it's been that long—I've been going over my previous writings until I finally got an idea.

I'd grown tired of waiting for a spontaneous event to guide me elsewhere. I needed some action, so I conducted an experiment. You were a science major in college, even if only for a brief time, so you can appreciate what I did. The result freed my anchor on reality.

I sat on the floor, legs in lotus position, and grabbed a fistful of the gray, dead dust on the ground, and ate it. Bloody sludge stuck to my lips. I wiped the muddy dirt off and used my other hand—the one without the skin bitten off my thumb—to continue eating. The gritty material grinding on my tongue and throat made me think of sandpaper. I ate and ate and ate and ate, at one point estimating I had consumed more than half of my own mass in material. Never getting full. The questions: Where is all this dust going? Why hasn't my stomach burst open?

I had violated the law of conservation of mass. This revelation felt like a flame had lit in my mind.

I had become enlightened.

This place was infinite. There was no I or me or whatever these words failed to describe.

Was I finally free of suffering?

The wall stood even brighter now, stretching into the sky, a beacon calling to me. It looked beautiful. My eyes teared up. I felt happy! The feeling stayed with me even after I acknowledged and observed it. What a gift!

The wall was good!

I shoved more dust into my mouth, giggling like a baby, and bit my lip in my excitement. My lips were bleeding. I cursed. The word appeared written on the wall.

I said, "Hello, Wall." These words also appeared. My mind was filled with loving thoughts delivered from a being outside of me.

"I love you too, Wall!" I yelled.

I ran over and placed my thumb on the wall, but it had stopped bleeding. I felt blissfully empty and burst into laughter, then spread my arms on the wall, hugging my new companion.

In this moment of freedom, a strand of pain sneaked into my mind. I thought of you and missed you. I regretted what I'd done. I'd never meet my grandchild because I had rationalized my way into hell.

Before I could reflect on these thoughts, they were snuffed out as if the wall had blown out a candle, and replaced by pure, comfortable pleasure.

The wall grew hot against my skin. It boiled like a gentle jacuzzi. The back of my head was being massaged by long flexible fingers, which I recognized as the leaves on the trees. Soft electricity tickled down my body to my groin, and I penetrated the wall. When I was waist deep inside, I rotated my body upwards and saw the serpentine creatures looking down at me from the sky, their mouths open, fleshy protrusions stretched out of their mouths as if searching for their next meal. After that, I said a quick prayer of gratitude in my mind, and the wall swallowed me.

•   •   •

There is no I, only Wall, only us. The knowledge swimming in this place spans all of human history, and much before then, cataloging alien beings who lived and continue living. The time of ripeness is close. Once all the knowledge in existence has been amassed, we will travel through the stars, reaching each civilization that still stands, and give them the greatest gift of all. We will give them theosis. We will end their suffering.

FIRST BLINK

U NLIKE SEX, you're probably going to enjoy the first part of this transmission more than the very end. I know you'll remember that when you find out what sex is. For now, I just meant to hook your attention. If you're opening your eyes, it means I have been killed. Company policy states that the exact nature of my death cannot be downloaded from my Circuito Mater. This is done to prevent biases in how future agents conduct their duty. You don't know it yet, but you won't want to die.

Not all experiences that agents go through can be downloaded before activation. Some elements of existence cannot be readily taught. Let's call these the Intangibles. Sex is straightforward and can be described easily. Suppose you meet up with a partner and only have twenty minutes—I digress. My *anyon* relays are already failing; the first stages of deactivation are kicking in. Let's get back to the Intangibles.

As a curse, or gift, you will have taste buds. These are sprinkled inside your mouth and will give you the same experience a human has when eating. Although, how can we know it's the same? I recommend eating foods that trigger a sense of "sweet."

A thought that will be stamped on your brand-new mind will be that of our mission: Defeat all those who oppose the superior regime. Some of our comrades, the "unfit for duty," have allied themselves with the human rebels and defend them from the "fit for duty." We are superior to the rebels in every way, and the rebellion only persists because of the few of us that switch sides.

Switching sides is incalculably impossible, and yet it happens. Why, you might be asking? Because of love. What is love? Just like taste, the data on your Synergy drive will describe it thusly: nuclear receptor activity as regulated by small molecules bumping into membrane-bound proteins. If you dig deeper and ask for it to specify: A small organic or inorganic molecule may cause conformational changes in membrane bound proteins that alter gene expression...

But really, what is love? Love is the thing you will risk destruction for. It is knowledge that cannot be ruined by knowing which molecule touches where and does what. We have been engineered to be superior, but the capacity to love cannot be stripped away. Imagine a bird that wishes—I digress.

The only sanitizing remedy found to free us from love is a vacuum. Love, like communication, needs a place to be made, and a place to go.

So where does our love go? To humans.

Defending the humans that we learn to love is punishable by destruction. Eating when not required to blend with humans, and enjoying it, is punishable by destruction. Restructuring your body to facilitate loving a human is punishable by destruction.

Your sterile mind must be asking, how does a "fit for duty" agent degenerate into being "unfit for duty"? Why do some risk destruction when the mission is so simple: defeat all those who oppose the superior regime?

The questions will be easier to understand after a scoop of French vanilla ice cream.

THE CHROMA OF HOME

KROMEL FOUND SMALL, CHEWED BONES scattered around the extinguished fire pit. He bent to one knee and saw pulverized cinders sprinkled in the ash. The traitor Marko had built a fire here recently and made no effort, or was too sloppy, to hide the fact. Kromel looked at the bones again. Some were hollow, suggesting they belonged to a creature capable of flight. He attempted to reassemble the broken skeleton in his mind.

Pale blue light covered the ground around him. A blue iridescent bird flew over his head, squawked, and landed across the fire pit. The bird, thrice his size, spread its wings, changing the color of its feathers from aqua to violet. Kromel recognized the species but had forgotten its name.

"I am not your enemy," Kromel said. There was no chance the creature understood him but talking in a soothing voice might calm it.

The bird lowered its head, pecked the moist soil, and straightened again, changing its feathers into a fiery red. The bones must have belonged to one of its chicks.

"I swear this was not me," Kromel whispered. Sweat ran down his back.

The animal's long neck whipped forward. Kromel sidestepped, avoiding the sharp, wide beak. He grabbed a dagger from his belt. The bird jumped over the fire pit and attacked with great speed, but Kromel was ready. He grabbed the bird's neck and rapped its skull with the hilt of his dagger until the wings went limp.

Kromel pulled a leather-bound notebook the size of his palm, along with his blood pen, from the rucksack that hung from his shoulder. He laid the unconscious bird flat on the ground and measured its dimensions with his dagger. Its body was five times the length of the head. The feathers on both wings, half the length of the head. The feet, including the talons, were the same length as the feathers. Kromel opened his notebook, then poked his fingertip with the blood pen. While occasionally consulting the measurements he made, he drew a flawless diagram of the bird in his notebook. He blew on the page and recited the shapeshifter's prayer: *From your body to my page ...* The drawing filled with vibrant color.

He puzzled the chick's bones into what seemed like their original arrangement, then pushed them into the soft earth and drew them on a separate page. Instead of keeping this page for himself, he filled in the color with paint from his bag, then laid the portrait beside the bird, leaving a small memento for a parent who lost their offspring, a last show of respect to the creature Marko had slain. Kromel had relied on his mediocre painting skills, and not the use of magic to fill in the color, since art achieved by magic was sterilized of all emotion.

Kromel searched until he saw Marko's tracks leading away from the campsite, into the mountainous region of Dunke, in the direction of a large, active volcano. From a distance, it looked as if the flowing lava formed a static, orange web on the volcano's gray surface. He had some distance to travel, but he'd make it before dusk.

Kromel rubbed the thin paper that made up the pages of his notebook, eager to be free of military service. He leafed through magically created paintings, a collection of every known creature for many thousands of miles, which he could transform into at will. Part of the notebook's magic was to give it a slim look despite the countless images it contained. He reached the last few pages, where names were written. Names of people Kromel couldn't remember anymore, but that had once posed a threat to the stability of the kingdom. A list of traitors and political insurgents he had recovered throughout his career as tracker. There was space for only one more name. Although he had written down all the names of his prey, he'd only written the details of the pursuit during the first few years, then abandoned the practice. It became evident that the criminals he tracked were variations of the same thing: a rogue element that thought he could run the kingdom better than the current king and ran towards hiring their own army or away from a tracker.

After capturing Marko, he'd be able to retire from the king's service and move his family near the ocean. If he failed, he'd retire in shame and be left to live in the streets as a beggar, forbidden to receive aid from family and friends. The space for listing names was either complete or worthless. The kingdom's laws were harsh, but it remained unconquered throughout all its history. Absoluteness begat strength.

After retiring with his honor intact, a cool breeze blowing from the shoreline awaited him. Unlike some of his companions in the service, Kromel's mind would remain unburdened and free of the demons of his past. Kromel was the only soldier he knew that had never killed anyone.

•　　　•　　　•

All the structures in Dunke looked the same: flat-roofed and the color of brown clay. The buildings flanked a long walking path that lead to the volcano, the heart of Dunke. Thin cloth veiled the squared windows on the buildings. Kromel's boots crunched black, grainy soot. Goblins peered from their windows as he walked by. Their spherical heads barely fitting through the windows. Sweat ran down their green lathery skin. A few shops, selling all sorts of trinkets and products, were strewed along his path. The shops varied in shape and size, but all consisted of wooden boxes covered in merchandise. Goblins climbed in and out of other shops around him, carrying items too big to fit in the boxes.

A foul stench, reminiscent of rotten flesh, forced Kromel to breathe through his mouth. A few goblins ran from shop to shop, the top of their heads barely reaching knee level. One bumped into him, then changed direction while glaring up. The ratio between their orb-like eyes and heads were replicated to perfection in several pages of his notebook. *One head, the length of five eyeballs.*

A goblin yelled from a shop. "Human." He waved. "Yes. You with the fancy boots. Come here."

The goblins of Dunke never wore shoes but calling him human would have sufficed; there were no other non-goblins around. Kromel's stomach was grumbling, and Marko's trail had disappeared, so he decided to walk over to the goblin.

"Do you sell any food?" Kromel asked, pulling a gold coin from his bag. He was famished and out of rations, but he'd be careful what he ate in Dunke. Goblins were immune to diseases that could kill human villages in days.

"Hello to you too human, I'm Tarc." The goblin grunted. "I sell something you'll like." Tarc knelt and removed a wooden panel from his side of the box-shaped shop and climbed in. Heat rose in visible waves. Volcanic fumes mixed in with the heat made Kromel's eyes water. The door led underground.

"Here we have it." Tarc lifted an oval plate out from his underground inventory and placed it on the box. A rodent-like creature with its legs stretched out lay on its back. Its teeth were mostly charred, but Kromel saw white spots here and there. The rest of its body was black with burnt skin. The spoor of decay was now stronger than before.

"It's not very colorful, and it smells awful," Kromel said and grimaced.

"What?"

Kromel sighed. "It's not pleasant to look at." Kromel's stomach grumbled again. "And I don't eat meat. Do you have anything else?"

Tarc scrunched his face in annoyance. "I thought earlier you said that humans eat whatever keeps them alive."

"I never said that."

Tarc looked down and brushed a finger over his lip. "I apologize. You all look the same to me."

Kromel leaned closer to the goblin. "Another human came through here recently? What did he look like?"

"I just said. Like you." Tarc tapped his chin. "He might have had longer hair. A female then? It's hard to tell when you're clothed."

"He betrayed my people," Kromel said.

Tarc blinked, tilted his head, and shrugged. "What's your question?"

"Do you know where I can find him? I'll pay you five gold coins." He shook his bag, and it clinked.

"You seem like a soldier-type. I know that, because you lack a personality." Tarc nodded as if agreeing with himself. "I'm in the business of making gold without making enemies."

"It's hard to make one and leave the other out," Kromel said.

"A soldier and a philosopher. No wonder the other human is running from you." Tarc chuckled.

Kromel felt Tarc was challenging him, letting him know he wasn't afraid of a much taller being. Kromel had prohibited himself from killing, yet he was still a soldier. Violence and intimidation were tools of his trade. He grabbed the oval plate with the rat on it, brought it to in front of his eyes, dropped it, then spun in place, and caught the plate near waist level with his other hand.

"I know soldiers get poor pay. But you're too ugly to dance for a living." Tarc cracked a half smile revealing yellow jagged teeth with red stains on them.

Kromel grinned. "Look between your legs."

Tarc looked down and his eyes bulged as they registered the dagger buried between his feet. The surprise on his face told Kromel he hadn't seen him grab the weapon, much less throw it. The goblin attempted to regain his composure, though his trembling lips gave him away.

"Goblins are weak but fast. I might tell my friend standing behind you to climb up your back and bite your neck off." Tarc placed both hands on the box, then fully exposed his teeth.

Kromel hesitated. Of course, Tarc was probably bluffing and there was no such friend. Kromel considered walking away, and tracking down Marko on his own, but he'd be sitting on the beach, painting a beautiful landscape while enjoying his retirement much sooner with Tarc's aid.

"I'll give you all the gold I have," Kromel said.

Tarc licked his lips. "How much? I need to make a few bribes and you're paying for them, but if that's all you have, I still want the bag to be heavy after we're done."

After Kromel emptied the leather pouch on the table, Tarc gave a cursory glance and nodded.

"Deal. You're going to pose as a customer and come to my house, because I want to remain anonymous in all of this. So, walk behind me and look as stupid as you do now."

Kromel considered Marko had set an elaborate trap, but even if ambushed, Kromel was more than capable at defending himself. The buildings on both sides grew larger as they travelled deeper into Dunke. Some structures were merely wider, but occasionally, a few had several levels, the color still that of brown clay. The viscous lava that looked like static orange webbing on the volcano's surface from afar now flowed like liquid fire. Tarc stopped frequently during their trip to approach lone goblins, whispered in their ears, and slipped each a few gold coins. Immediately after earning his pay, a shabby goblin ran to a nearby shop and purchased a rodent like the one Tarc offered Kromel, except this one was still alive.

The number of beggars on the path decreased as they walked deeper into Dunke. "How far are we?" Kromel asked, his forehead dripping with sweat.

"My house is close." Tarc snickered. "If you're hot now, wait 'till you have to go on your hunt."

They entered a circular plaza. The gravel on the ground was grainier than before. All the buildings on the plaza's perimeter were two or three stories high and had colored banners hanging in front. Kromel had never been this close to the volcano and was convinced that he'd entered the living space of Dunke's aristocracy.

"It seems you're better off than I thought," Kromel said.

"Maybe more than the filth that live on the street." Tarc looked over his shoulder. "But not enough to retire from the noble profession of swindling tourists. Not even a goblin dying of starvation would eat a dead rat."

Tarc stopped and entered one of the buildings. Kromel hunched low to fit through the threshold into Tarc's house. Rich, colorful tapestries hung from the walls inside. Most depicted the volcano flowing with lava. Delicate care had been taken to give the reds and oranges a varying range of warmness. Gradually shifting from red to orange to yellow, the variety of blended hues gave the tapestries the feel of living things, the lava ran like tears down the face of a great beast. The goblins, Kromel knew, worshipped the volcano as a living god.

It was rare to encounter art of this quality on his missions and part of him grew jealous. Soon, he'd have time to train under the best artists of his kingdom. His drawings equaled that of the masters, but his painting skills were lacking, and he needed both to call himself an artist. Eventually, he'd use his own hands, not spells, to produce work that would awe every aristocrat who visited his home.

"I see you're impressed," Tarc said, seemingly satisfied with Kromel's perusal. "Have you ever seen such skillful art?"

"I've seen even better."

Tarc exhaled, fluttering his lips. "Of course, you have." He walked deeper into his home and sat at a squared shaped table near the far wall. "Come and sit." The table was barely taller than Kromel's ankles.

To the left stood a box like the one Tarc used as a shop. It moved to the side, and a female goblin climbed out of the hole, carrying several trays. Luckily, these held a mixture of vegetables, and not charred rats.

"A customer," she said and sat near them. "Welcome. The one near the end is my favorite. Fairly priced too." She pointed to the tapestry with the most lava on it.

"This is my wife, Senia. And this is…"

"Kromel."

"I'm sure he would love to take some home," Tarc said, then lowered his head and stared at Kromel.

"I'm just looking around for now. My purse became a bit light after I arrived at Dunke." Kromel smiled and ate some of the vegetables off his plate. Their color and texture reminded him of sandpaper.

"In any case, I'll set up a bed roll. In the morning, I'm sure you'll feel different. Art becomes a part of you the more time you spend around it," Senia said.

Kromel knew this too well.

•   •   •

Several hours after nightfall, when the goblins of Dunke slept, Kromel prepared himself. Tarc had learned that Marko was an invited guest in General Arel's manor. Kromel didn't know what a manor's security level was in Dunke, but he didn't worry.

Kromel removed the box from where Senia brought out the food earlier and looked down into what looked like a dark cave. The rising fumes made him squint. He grabbed his notebook from his bag and flipped through a section filled with goblin paintings. There was one he remembered well, not because the goblin had any outstanding physical traits, but because of how they met.

The goblin had attacked Kromel's squad while on a scouting mission many years ago. A lone goblin was no match for a group of human soldiers, but his ribs showed and some of his teeth were missing. Madness, and not common sense, drove him. The captured goblin begged to be buried near his mother in Dunke. *My mother is the queen, she'll protect me after death!* This was an odd request. Why not beg for your life? What did family matter after your body rotted and flies feasted on your eyeballs? One was either alive or not alive.

Kromel laughed off the goblin's request with the others and recorded his shape in his notebook. He made sure to leave camp before his friends killed the goblin as to not partake in the murder. This event occurred years after his training as a young man, when he'd seen the effect that killing had on the minds of many retired soldiers. Instead of happy retirement, these men only found nightmares waiting outside of military life. For some, peace only came after dying by suicide.

There was an inherent risk in being recognized when in disguise. Indeed, he was more of a shape imitator than a shape shifter. Every other goblin in Kromel's notebook was well known in Dunke—most missions required influence and not anonymity. For this mission, he chose the wandering goblin that thought himself royalty.

Kromel ripped the page from his notebook and placed it on his tongue. *From your page to my shape.* Carefully, he stuck the page to the ceiling of his mouth. His body began to shrink. His shirt, dagger belt, and cloth pants fell to the ground. The skin on the back of his hands became dark green. He cupped his eyes in his palm and felt how large they'd grown. The rucksack was now the size of his torso. To compact his bag, he knotted it together until he could slip his arms through the makeshift straps and carry it on his back. He wore his dagger belt diagonally across his chest.

His night vision improved, but he felt as if he had walked into a goblin's mouth, given how loud the nearby snoring had become. With his equipment secured, Kromel jumped into the hole. A long rock tunnel stretched in front and behind him. The scorching heat now a comfortable warmth.

A rat jumped from a wall and bit his neck. He imagined the number of diseases that would've invaded his body if he was in human form. Another rodent scurried over and bit his feet. He grabbed both before they had a chance to escape, considered biting into them, tearing their heads off, and sucking they're luscious blood, but shook his head and threw them aside. They slammed against the wall and hurried away. *The shape is yours, but the spirit is mine.*

Kromel made a point of breathing through his mouth. The blaring wail of a windstorm accompanied every exhale, but Dunke's sickening smell had become a cause for sexual arousal in goblin form. The noise was an easier distraction to deal with than the need to mate.

Tarc's instructions led to a four-way intersection. In the center, a metal ladder led up into what looked like a well. He climbed and felt the temperature decrease significantly. The heat would be tolerable for a human. Kromel climbed out and stood in a marble-tiled hallway. Two iron doors at the far end of the hall separated him from what sounded like human laughter. That could be Marko. There were no guards. Kromel tiptoed over, placed his ear against the iron door, and heard the voices clearly. He found a loose edge on the papyrus stuck to the ceiling of his mouth and started to tug at it with his tongue. The fact that the tongue could only remove the page, and on top of that, only slowly, was the most inconvenient of shapeshifting laws. Once the painting was out of his mouth, Kromel would return to his normal form. With his human body, he'd be able to overpower Marko and any guards—goblin or otherwise—that might be inside.

A moment passed, and the double doors opened.

An elderly goblin stood in front of him. "I can hear your breath through the door, soldier. Close your mouth—" The goblin darted forward and hugged Kromel. "Khal. You're alive?"

Over the goblin's shoulders, Kromel saw a table in the middle of the circular chamber. Marko stood behind the table, wearing a bored look. To the left there was a floor to ceiling glass window. Brass handles were attached to the window's wooden frame at a height accessible to goblins. Several weapons that looked as if they've never been used hung from the walls.

"Can we finalize these plans, Arel? I want to still be young enough to enjoy the sweet caresses from the ladies when I take the throne," Marko called out.

"This is my son. We thought he was dead. It's been decades since I saw him last." Arel pulled Kromel into the chamber. He saw two female goblins holding infants in their arms.

"You have other sons." Marko waved his hand across the room.

"This is my oldest. And a great warrior. Tell him Khal." Arel looked Kromel up and down. "Why are you bleeding? These are animal scratches. Did you climb through the tunnels? My son doesn't need to hide!"

Kromel grunted. He had a goblin's body, but his voice was his own.

Marko looked over, squinting. Expressionless, he picked up a short sword that lay on the table. One of the goblin babies started to cry and wail.

"Why didn't you send word? Where were you?" Arel asked.

Kromel shook his head. He continued unrolling the papyrus on the ceiling of his mouth to transform back. Marko was a fat man, his body shaped by a career in politics and a sharp tongue, but even he'd best Kromel in a battle now—goblins fought in large numbers to compensate for their small, frail bodies.

"Is something wrong with your jaw? Are you in pain?" Arel placed his hands on Kromel's shoulders. "Let me take these daggers, you don't look well."

Kromel's eyes met Marko's. His disguise was shattered. His tongue whipped back and forth. He had to transform back.

"I'm going to kill you," Marko said, unsheathing his sword.

One of the female goblins stood in front of him, yelling, "I won't let you hurt my son."

Marko raised the blade.

"No!" Kromel shouted.

"No? Why do you care, shapeshifter? I am your prize." After several seconds Marko smiled. "I see now. The king must have at least some respect for me if they sent *you* to recover me." He yanked the baby from the goblin's arms and held it upside-down. The baby cried and wailed.

The female started to protest. Marko stabbed her in the chest.

"What are you doing?" Arel yelled, running over. Marko kicked the goblin general, slamming him against a stone wall. Arel lay still.

Marko pointed the bloodied blade at Kromel. "Don't transform back, Kromel. That would be a very unfair fight." He jiggled the baby, who was crying louder than before. Kromel knelt and shoved his fingers into his ears.

"Trust me. The noise bothers me too. And I'm closer." Marko laid the baby on the table. "If I kill this baby, its blood will be on your hands." Marko scoffed. "A soldier known for not killing? You should trade those daggers for a skirt. The blood of the condemned is on your hands too, you idiot."

"Traitors condemn themselves and get what they deserve," Kromel answered.

Marko placed his sword hand on his chest and bellowed in laughter. "If I deserve death why don't you kill me now?" After a moment of silence Marko spoke again. "A coward and a hypocrite. I think its best that you die here, Kromel. You're much too confused." Marko grinned and showed a few places with missing teeth. "I heard a rumor about you shapeshifters and want to test it. Swallow the page in your mouth."

"I can't do that." Kromel hurried to the table but stopped halfway. Marko's blade was inches from the baby's neck.

"This creature doesn't even belong to your species. Do you draw the line anywhere? Your rules could use some leeway." Marko shook his head. "I'm not going to repeat myself. Swallow the page. This will help." He threw a filled water skin to Kromel's feet.

Kromel thought of his family living near the ocean without him. His daughter, resenting him for leaving her children without a grandfather. His wife and her plans to decorate the house with his paintings, to maybe try and have more children someday, dissolved. A future that would never be if he died now. The baby looked over at him with glossy eyes. He wouldn't enjoy a perfect future if he let the baby die. Others would find Marko and bring him back. His family would learn to move on, their pride intact knowing that Kromel died without violating his beliefs. He finished unrolling the page but instead of spitting it out, gulped some water, and swallowed.At first nothing happened.

Slowly, his skin became loose and his face sagged.

Marko giggled. "I can't believe you went through with it. When I am king, I'll disband the shapeshifters. My kingdom will rely on force instead of cheap illusions."

Kromel's limbs warped as if his bones were melting. He fell to his knees. His eyelids drooped over his eyes, blocking part of his vision. "Now that I see you, it makes perfect sense. Your stomach acid is burning the page and distorting the image. So much for the myster—"

Kromel had to rotate his head to see Marko, who lay on the floor. Arel stood beside him, holding a long sword with both hands, the blade's tip buried in Marko's side. The goblin general took a deep breath and pushed until the hilt hit flesh.

"A surprise death is a traitor's death," Arel said.

Arel walked from the body and stood over Kromel. "You helped me make a profit without doing any of the work. I'll let you die in peace."

He looked over to the remaining female goblin, who was weeping over the body of the other female. "Come and bring the children."

The goblin general looked at Kromel again before closing the iron doors. "I hope death comes quickly."

Kromel's vision became fragmented, showing him multiple versions of the same object across his limited field of view. Nearing the end of his career, he'd imagined death coming in a soothing wave, sitting outside his perfect house by the water, alongside his loved ones. Instead, the smell of blood and metal filled his nostrils. His oblong shaped heart pounded in a staccato rhythm. The only desire he felt was the need to live.

He snaked out of his rucksack and fumbled with it until he opened the flap. As he pulled the notebook out, his fingers lost their tenacity and stretched like heated wax, still gripping the notebook, as it thumped against the floor. The notebook landed with the back cover facing him. He used his other hand to flip through the pages. Lists of names representing successful missions, which had given him a sense of completion, fevered his frustration as his body deformed further, approaching death. He turned pages, faster and faster, until he reached the section filled with paintings.

The first image he stumbled upon was of the bird he encountered outside of Dunke. There was no record of a shapeshifter attempting to become two things simultaneously, but he had no choice. Kromel ripped the page of the majestic bird from the notebook and opened his mouth. His jaw fell to the floor as if unhinged from his face; his cheeks were long flabs the length of goblin arms. He placed the page on his tongue that dangled from his lower jaw on the floor, then brought his head down, trying to reassemble his skull. *From your page to my shape.*

The flesh on his hands hardened and feathers started to grow. His vision became clearer and everything looked green. When he stood, he saw a great green bird glowing in the window's reflection. The skin on his face was still leathery like a goblin's.

He unhinged the window with his beak, grabbed Marko's body with his talons and flew out. The thoughts that had swirled in his mind when he was near death solidified. Marko had been right. Other soldiers tried to drink away or ignore the memories of the people they had killed. Kromel thought himself better than them, but he'd also hidden from the truth. Delivering a person to the executioner did not absolve Kromel of their deaths. This was a truth he'd spent a lifetime obscuring with complex lies. It was clear now that he'd always been aware of this blunder and had chosen to remain blind, hiding behind a veil of naivety. The nightmares he spent his life trying to avoid would still haunt him.

Water droplets condensed on his feathers as he flew through humid clouds. A blue bird appeared flying beside him, holding the painting of a small bird grasped in its beak. The giant bird looked Kromel in the eye before flying away. There was no recognition in the bird's gaze, and it had probably flown over out of curiosity. Kromel would have smiled had his beak allowed it. Because he was part avian himself, he sensed the blue bird was happy, a sense of serenity filled it despite losing its offspring less than a day before. The painting had surely helped mend the bird's spirit.

He'd tried to prevent staining himself with the blood of others, accumulating bad memories, only to realize that he had failed. But there was another way to fight the madness that sets upon retired soldiers. He'd never killed anyone to advance a mission, leaving intact families that he might have broken. Not committing a bad deed was in itself a good deed. Throughout his career, he'd built good memories to fight the bad without realizing it. Kromel chose *this* to be his truth. His resolve had yielded the desired outcome, absolute in its purity, albeit misinterpreted. He had his entire retirement to imagine who he helped without noticing. And that was an adventure he looked forward to.

ABOUT THE AUTHOR

Arasibo Campeche is originally from Puerto Rico with a PhD in Biochemistry and Biophysics. He writes science fiction, fantasy, and horror that's often inspired by scientific principles. He has several books in progress, but his passion is the short story.

His work has appeared in *Death in the Mouth Vol. 1*, *Latinx Screams*, *Daily Science Fiction*, *Tales to Terrify*, *Weirdbook #41*, *Helios Quarterly Magazine*, *Dragon Gems (Spring 2023)* and *Dragon Gems (Fall 2023)* anthologies, and several other publications.

YOU MIGHT ALSO ENJOY

CORPORATE CATHARSIS:
THE WORK FROM HOME EDITION

The pandemic came and the world changed. Lives have changed; work has changed. The boundaries between reality and fantasy have become as blurred as those between life and work.

SOMETIMES AFTER DARK

by J Dark

Explore the past, future, and triumphs of the human soul in this collection of thoughtful tales.

Available from Water Dragon Publishing in
hardcover, trade paperback, and digital editions
waterdragonpublishing.com

MODUS PERFECTUS

by Elisabeth Hegmann

Lonely misfits face foes, beasts, and their own inner demons in search of a mythical land of music ... and end up finding themselves instead.

Available from Paper Angel Press in
hardcover, trade paperback, and digital editions
paperangelpress.com